Also by Kate Gallison

BURY THE BISHOP
DEVIL'S WORKSHOP
UNHOLY ANGELS
HASTY RETREAT

GRAVE
MISGIVINGS

GRAVE MISGIVINGS

A Mother Lavinia Grey Mystery

Kate Gallison

Delacorte Press

Published by
Delacorte Press
Bantam Doubleday Dell Publishing Group, Inc.
1540 Broadway
New York, New York 10036

This novel is a work of fiction. Names, characters, places, and incidents either are the product of the author's imagination or are used fictitiously. Any resemblance to actual persons, living or dead, events, or locales is entirely coincidental.

Library of Congress Cataloging in Publication Data
Gallison, Kate.
    Grave misgivings : a Mother Lavinia Grey mystery / by Kate
Gallison.
        p.   cm.
    ISBN 0-385-31929-0
    I. Title.
PS3557.A414G35   1998
813'.54—dc21   98-7331
                                                        CIP

Manufactured in the United States of America
Published simultaneously in Canada

October 1998

10 9 8 7 6 5 4 3 2 1

For Lee Parks

Acknowledgments

Thanks to Roger Aspeling, a great lover of cemeteries, for the tour of Mount Hope, and to the ever-knowledge-able Bill Waits, and to the folks who shared their flood stories with me. Thanks to Peggy Schenck for lending me her copy of *The Great Flood Disaster of 1955*.

1

"Tell me again what you were doing in the cemetery in the rain," Mother Grey said.

The man and his daughter looked at each other, a glance just this side of conspiracy and guilt. Their shaking blue hands tightened on Mother Grey's best teacups. The handle of a small collapsible spade was clearly visible among the contents of the daughter's canvas bookstore tote bag, and for a moment Mother Grey thought the worst.

They both spoke at once: "We were looking for my father." "We were looking for my grandfather."

"You might have waited for better weather," she suggested mildly. On her way back from saying the burial service over Hester Winkle in a freezing rainstorm, Mother Grey had found these two wandering through

1

the Mount Outlook Cemetery, dressed for the weather in Phoenix, Arizona, where they said they came from. Naturally she had rescued them and brought them home to the rectory.

Their sodden shoes, stuffed with newspapers, rested by the back door. Their porous jackets hung dripping over the back of the extra kitchen chair, and their shivering laps each held a warm animal—Towser, the dog, on the man's lap, Scratch, the cat, on the young woman's. But Mother Grey was having trouble making sense of their story. "I thought you said you were looking for your grandmother."

"Oh, no," said the young woman, Shannon her name was. "We have Nana with us."

"A blessing," said Mother Grey. "Older family members are such a—"

"I mean she's right here," said Shannon. She pushed the dark wet curls out of her eyes, stuck her hand into the tote bag, and pulled out a box made of bronze-colored imitation leather, roughly the size of a shoebox but wider, deeper, and shorter. "Nana's ashes are in this box. The one we were looking for in the cemetery was my grandfather." She took the cat by the fur of its cheeks and touched her nose to its nose. "Pretty kitty! . . . They would have been married fifty years next month. We came to bury her ashes next to him."

"I see." Now Mother Grey remembered hearing her say something like "I've lost my grandfather," which Mother Grey had misunderstood to mean the grandfather had just died. "How long has your grandfather been gone?"

"Forty years," Shannon said.

"I thought sure we'd find him up in St. Joseph's

graveyard," said the father, whose name was . . .
Marty? Mark. His skin was like his daughter's, pale underneath the freckles, but the shape of his face was different. The family resemblance was all in the eyes.

"My mother was such a devout Catholic that I assumed my father was too," Mark said, as Mother Grey
refilled his teacup. "But we looked everywhere. Then we
thought maybe not, so we started to look for him where
the non-Catholics were buried."

The cemetery of the Church of St. Joseph the Worker
was on the very crest of Mount Outlook, commanding a
view of Bucks County and the Delaware River valley that
was the envy of many a New Jersey developer. Mother
Grey had been reliably informed that one of them had
actually had the nerve to approach Father de Spain with
bundles of money and a proposal to move the headstones, the crosses, the statues of angels, and all the
graves down to a lot the developer owned in the flood-
plain.

"The view up there," he had argued, "is wasted on the
dead." To his credit, Father de Spain had refused indig-
nantly, or so it was said. It was true that St. Joseph's was
not suffering the same sort of fiscal insecurity as St.
Bede's, Mother Grey's little mission church.

Mount Outlook, below St. Joseph's fence, was the
other graveyard, the burying ground for Fishersville's
Protestants and other non-Catholics. The view from their
plots was also quite fine. Some of the Protestant dead
had been rich industrialists and lay in mausoleums big
enough to be seen from the valley—the Wagonners, the
Greens. (The Wagonners were in umbrellas; where the
Greens had made their money, Mother Grey hadn't
heard. She was still a newcomer in Fishersville, there a

mere seven years.) If not for a few intervening houses and evergreen trees, Mother Grey would have been able to gaze right out her living-room window at the ten-foot-high monument to the Wagonners, for the Mount Outlook Cemetery was an inescapable presence looming over the southeast corner of Fishersville. Made the townspeople think. Some of them, anyway.

When the weather was good, Mother Grey had been known to go up there on no particular errand, partly because walking up the hill was such good exercise and partly because to read the gravestones helped her understand the history of her adopted hometown. But on a day like this, nothing but a funeral would have caused her to climb Mount Outlook, and nothing at all would have induced her to walk. The last snowstorm of April had come pelting down in gobs of slush, followed closely by a hard rain. Toiling back to her car afterward through ankle-deep nastiness, she had come upon this young woman on the steps of the Wagonner mausoleum, drenched and sniffling.

The father had appeared then, looking even sorrier than the daughter. Nothing stood between his graying head and the fury of the elements, not even a baseball cap. A drip—she thought it was rain—hung off the end of his snub nose.

Mother Grey, in her role as protector of strays, had gathered them both up and taken them home with her to get dry and warm. The story they unfolded to her grew more and more strange. Nana? In a shoebox?

"How is it," Mother Grey asked the man, "that you don't know for certain what your father's religion was?"

"I was very young when he died," he said. "Only six."

"Ah." Mother Grey, too, had been quite young when

her parents were killed in an auto accident. There were many things she would never know about them, some of them probably important. But at least she knew where they were buried. "So you've never seen your father's grave?"

"Reverend, I haven't even seen the state of New Jersey in forty years."

"My word," she said. "I take it you grew up in the West."

"Grew up, went to college, lived my entire life. My mother talked about Fishersville all the time, and yet in forty years she never once went back. My wife used to tease her. She made fun of Fishersville, called it Fishtown."

"Your wife. Did you leave her back in Phoenix?"

He sighed miserably. "She's gone," he said.

Run away? Passed on? Resting in a shoebox somewhere? "I'm so sorry," Mother Grey said.

"Mom died when I was little," Shannon said.

"I'm sorry to hear it." Mother Grey took a mouthful of tea and put her cup down. Her own grandmother's cup. It clinked in the saucer. "What do you do, Mr. Smith?"

"I'm a computer consultant. I run a small company. We specialize in year-two-thousand problems."

"What problems are those?"

"When the year two thousand comes, it will create problems for many computing systems. We attempt to anticipate what these will be and minimize damage."

"But what will you do for a living after the year two thousand?" she blurted, thinking after the words were out how tactless they sounded.

"Hard to say. What will you do for a living after the

Second Coming?" A joke. He flashed a smile, transforming his face; his teeth were beautiful.

"So what do you think, Reverend Grey? How can we find my grandfather's grave?" Shannon asked.

Finding a lost grave. "You need to talk to Father de Spain," Mother Grey said. "They keep records at St. Joseph's of deaths and burials."

"He might even remember," said Shannon.

"Oh, no, not him. He's younger than I am, and I myself wasn't born until the year after that flood," said Mother Grey. "It was in 1955, wasn't it? There are still some old-timers in town who might remember your family."

"But we have no relatives here," Mark said.

"I mean from before," Mother Grey said. "Someone might know something that would help you."

"Daddy, you don't suppose we have relatives in the area, do you?"

"Your grandmother never told me, if we do."

"She had an old boyfriend in town. You knew that, didn't you, Daddy?"

"What was his name?" Mother Grey asked.

"John."

"Last name?"

"She never said."

That should be easy enough; there couldn't be more than three or four hundred old men in the county named John.

"Nana told you about her old boyfriends?" Mark said.

"Nana told me all sorts of things about her life in the olden days, before you were born."

"Did she talk about your grandfather?"

"Not much, no. Talking about him seemed to be painful to her."

"Well, what, then?" Mark was having trouble with the notion that his mother might have had a life worth talking about before he was born, a life apart from even his father.

"Old times in Fishersville," Shannon said. "Making fudge. Pulling taffy. Hayrides in the country. Sledding on Reeker's Hill."

"Oh. Those old days."

"And of course the war, when your dad was away. She knew I wanted to be a writer, so she told me a lot of things. She wanted me to know all about life-with-a-capital-L. She used to describe this town so much, I feel as though I've been here before."

"So how do you like it?" Mother Grey said. "Does it meet your expectations?"

"It's charming," Shannon said. "I love the little houses all close together, and the porches with the Victorian gingerbread. It's so historic. We don't have anything as old as that in the West. But the weather is wet here, isn't it?"

Mother Grey smiled. "Compared to Phoenix, I suppose it is," she said.

"Wet," Mark said. "Yes. When my mother and I left here . . ." As his voice trailed off, he seemed to be staring way inside himself.

"Was it raining?" Mother Grey prompted.

"I can't remember. Actually I think the sun was shining. But most of the town was under water."

"You must have left town during the great flood." People in town still spoke of the great flood of 1955 after all these years. Only last week a homeowner stripping wallpaper from his living-room wall had found a high-water mark on the plaster underneath, at the level of his chin. It was reported in the *Clarion*. "Do you remember what the flood was like?"

"Yes," he said, but his attention had turned inward. The response was automatic, the way you'd say any old thing just to keep people from interrupting your thoughts.

Mother Grey couldn't help prodding him anyway. It was the professional counselor in her. "How long was that after your father died?"

"I don't know. Five minutes. Half an hour. A week. I can't remember." He rubbed his hand over his stubbly hair. "I can't remember much of anything from those days." He gazed into the middle distance, seeing they knew not what, then spoke with startling vehemence: "I hate Fishersville."

The dog jumped off his lap. Shannon stared at him. "Daddy! I thought you wanted to come here and see your old hometown again."

"The sentimental journey to Hell," he said. "No, little sweetheart, I just want to get my mother planted in the ground and get out of here."

Mark Smith really could not understand why these women seemed to expect him to be in transports of delight over coming back to Fishersville. What was the town to him? He had been six years old when he left. If anything interesting had happened to him here, he couldn't remember it. He found himself looking at his hands. They seemed strangely large, even swollen. This very kitchen was like the kitchen of the house where he had lived as a boy. The stove was like his mother's old stove. Snippets of memory came and teased him, only to disappear again. He suffered from increasing discomfort, almost dread. Why had he come back to this town? When could he leave?

The memories of young childhood have a spooky quality, the more so if you've moved away from the remembered place where you were small. Buried in Mark's mind were little scenes, and sometimes at the smell of a food or a flower or the sound of a seldom-heard piece of music, one of these memories would pop out, whole and undigested, into his conscious mind. At such times he was inclined to try to analyze it. Now, as an adult, he knew events had meaning.

Fishersville pelted him with so many of these moments that he was nearly paralyzed with stupefaction. Simply by coming here, by driving through the town, he was bombarded: a picnic he and his mother had enjoyed on that hill, when the grass looked and smelled just so. (Who was that man with them? It was his dad, right?) A friend who had lived in such-and-such a house. Faces, voices, petunias in a front yard, the way an old woman wore pin curls in her hair.

He remembered his mother as she was in those days, slim, beautiful, her dark fluffy hair framing a lovely face that was often smiling. He remembered his little self, what he had looked like getting out of the claw-footed bathtub, his face in the mirror with its white skin and rosy cheeks, grimacing as he tried to grease and comb his hair into the knifelike ridge that was required by the nuns. Hairs would escape to fall in his eyes, and Sister Charles would send notes home to his mother about it. When she came to school to see his teachers, the other children used to admire his mother's looks. "Your mother's pretty," they said.

He remembered his father as a god.

Strangely, Mark couldn't remember his face. He remembered his tall large build and his hands, square and capable. But whenever he tried to think of his father's face, he was able to visualize only the framed photograph by his mother's bedside, a formal portrait in his army uniform. *What was your father like? He was gray. He wore an overseas cap. He was a god.*

In Mark's memory, his father had died suddenly on the night of the flood, the same night he and his mother had left Fishersville, never to return. But that couldn't have been. It takes time to bury a spouse and pack up a household, even the few things that might be left undamaged by the water. They must have been here long enough to see the river go down again.

Yes, they must have stayed on for some days, from the things he remembered. Mud everywhere, firemen pumping incessantly, smelly brown water out, with little fish and tadpoles, clean water in, clean water out again. Supper at the Baptist church, Red Cross ladies in flowered dresses. Sleeping on a floor. Lining up with other weeping children for typhoid shots.

Mark had not spoken of these things in forty years. Now that he tried to recall them, he found that his memories of leaving Fishersville, and even of the time before that, were filled with large strange holes. Why had his father died so young? How was it that his mother had never returned to Fishersville?

Why hadn't he asked her about it while she was still alive?

Maybe he had. Maybe she had reacted badly. There

were a number of subjects that had caused her to turn cold and shut him out, and he had learned over the years never to mention them. But he couldn't remember ever saying anything about—was it even important? What was he doing back here in Fishersville?

"What was the flood like?" Mother Grey asked him. "Do you remember anything about it?"

"It was hot. It was wet. I was six years old; I don't remember."

A smell—face powder, cigarettes, perfume. Hair tickling his face. His mother bending over to wake him in the night: *Markie, get up, the water is coming.*

Where's Dad?

Your father is dead.

2

Father de Spain, the priest at the Church of St. Joseph the Worker, was too young to have been in Fishersville at the time of the flood; Shannon saw that at once. He probably wasn't even born yet. And not only was he young, he was cute. She found herself meditating on the romantic possibilities of a story about falling in love with a priest. She hadn't written a story in about a month and a half. Good plots didn't come to her all that often.

"I'm looking for the grave of my father, James Smith," Shannon's father explained to the priest.

"He was buried in St. Joseph's cemetery?"

"We thought so, but we can't find the grave. He died in 1955."

Father de Spain offered to check the record of burials to see what he could see. Shannon leaned over his shoulder. The priest's scent was that of some subtle cologne. "There's no record whatever here of the burial of James Smith," he said. "Not at any time in 1955. Are you sure your father was a Roman Catholic, Mr. Smith?"

"My mother always said so."

"Perhaps he was buried from another church. If you like, I can write to Trenton."

"Father Angleford was here then," Mark said. "If we could talk to him, maybe he would know something."

The priest sighed. "John Angleford. Many people here still remember Father John, but he's long gone, I'm afraid. Went to his reward sometime in the sixties." John Angleford. John. Could it be that the dead priest was Mary Agnes's old love? Shannon's heart leaped at the potential for flaming romance. That would explain a lot about Nana, why she never remarried, carrying the torch all these years for a totally unobtainable man. But surely she would have mentioned it. She told Shannon everything. They had been like girlfriends.

"I'm sure when he was here, though, he would have maintained the church's records. We have no record of your father's funeral, or of his death."

He put the record of burials back on a shelf, next to a number of other well-worn record books. Then he pulled another one down and opened it on the desk. "One of the functions of the Church is to keep records," he said, as he began to page through the book. "As I'm sure you know. Maybe there will be something else."

"Surely there will be," Mark said.

"Ah! here we have his baptismal record," said the priest. Shannon leaned over his shoulder again and saw that her grandfather had been baptized on September

14

12, 1923. She tried to imagine it, Baby Grandfather in a long lace dress, his parents and godparents in silent-movie clothes. "And this looks like the record of his marriage to your mother in June 1947." The picture Shannon envisioned changed; now it was in Technicolor, and it was Nana who wore the white dress and a little hat with a spritz of white veil. That was a real picture she had seen in Nana's album. The original, of course, had been in black and white. People didn't take color pictures in 1947.

Mark said, "Why is there a line through it?" Sure enough, a line ran through the entry recording the marriage, a very thin line drawn with a fountain pen.

"I can't imagine," said Father de Spain.

Mother Grey was startled to see the two of them standing on her doorstep again. It seemed to her that scarcely an hour had passed. She had so much to do, and yet here they were. "Hi," said Shannon. "Can we come in?"

"By all means," Mother Grey said.

"Your Father de Spain wasn't a whole lot of use," Mark said.

"He was really cute, but as you said, he wasn't even born when Grandfather died, and he told us the priest who was here then has gone to his reward."

"The big cathedral in the sky," Mark muttered.

Shannon glared at him. "In any case he looked through all his records for us. He was sure that Grandfather was never buried from St. Joseph's," Shannon said.

"As for me, I'm ready to pack it in and go home," Mark said. "But Shannon—"

"Father de Spain suggested we look harder in the

other cemetery," Shannon said. "He told us the Mount Outlook Cemetery Association has those records, but there isn't a listing for them in the phone book. He couldn't remember who the members were, and he thought you might know."

Mother Grey had to think for a minute. Who were the members of the Mount Outlook Cemetery Association? The funeral director, of course, who took a professional interest, but there were others, including—Ah! "Delight van Buskirk," she said. Mrs. van Buskirk was St. Bede's oldest living parishioner, still sharp enough to serve on the vestry, still active in a number of other Fishersville institutions, including the cemetery association. "Let me give Mrs. van Buskirk a call. If she doesn't remember your family, she will at least know who has the cemetery map."

Mrs. van Buskirk's granddaughter answered the phone after the third ring. It must be her day to go over and clean. In the background Mother Grey could hear New Age harp music playing, light twinkly pap that revolted her aesthetic soul. *I ought to take that child in hand, introduce her to some real music.* Of course as a nonchurchgoer, she was out of range of Mother Grey's grip. "It's Mother Grey. May I speak to your grandmother?"

"Just a minute," the girl said. "Gra-*am!*"

Delight van Buskirk greeted Mother Grey cordially. She had the map herself, she said, and the other cemetery records as well. "It may not be as accurate as we'd like, the Mount Outlook Cemetery Association is doing a big project to update their records. We're finding contradictions. But you're welcome to come over and look at it."

"When can we come?"

"Right now would be fine."

"Thank you so much," Mother Grey said. "We'll see you in about ten minutes." She hung up the phone. "Mrs. van Buskirk has the map," she said. "If your father's grave is in Mount Outlook Cemetery, we'll know in the next half hour."

Shannon looked at the tote bag, and at her father's expressionless face. "But what if the grave isn't there?" she said.

"Then we can try talking to some of the old-timers in town," Mother Grey said. "The people who were here in 1955."

The rental car that the Smiths were driving was a new four-door with a lot more vim than Mother Grey's old Nova. She went with them to Mrs. van Buskirk's house, more or less as a guide. To get to Delight van Buskirk's farmhouse, hand-built by her grandfather more than a hundred years ago, one had to negotiate the knotted streets and cul-de-sacs of Fishers Pointe Victorian Towne-Homes, an infestation of new condos that now stood where the cows used to graze.

Mrs. van Buskirk opened the kitchen door to them and let out a blast of baking smells. In the months since Mother Grey last visited, the old lady's house had changed in some subtle way, quite apart from the relative height of Mrs. van Buskirk to the door frame. *Delight is getting shorter*, Mother Grey thought, and then, *Good grief. There are crystals and bunches of herbs all over the place.*

Furthermore the house was spotless—unusual for the home of a nonagenarian with failing eyesight. "Is Claudine living with you now?" Mother Grey asked.

"Yes, bless her," the old lady said. "My life is so much easier. She cooks, she cleans, she does everything. I don't know how I'm going to manage when she leaves."

Mother Grey made introductions. Granddaughter Claudine puttered around the kitchen table, shaking out the checkered tablecloth, laying the cups and saucers, pouring hot water into the teapot. She and Shannon Smith were of an age but nothing alike; Shannon, freckled and wholesome; Claudine, pale and ethereal, adorned with jewelry bearing pagan religious symbols, and in her nose a single gold bead. Bunches of dried green vegetable matter hung over the doorways. Bowls of crystals rested on every conceivable flat surface. Mother Grey found herself wondering what Delight van Buskirk, an honest Christian, made of all this.

Claudine produced a plate of fragrant muffins and then excused herself and retired to the other room, saying she had to study.

Delight poured the tea. "Would you like milk or lemon?"

It had been a long time since Mother Grey partook of Delight van Buskirk's cooking. Too long. The crisp buttery crust of the muffins gave way to a tender yet lightly textured—textured? "These are oat bran muffins, aren't they?" Mother Grey demanded.

"Yes, dear. They're very good for you."

"Health food, Mrs. van Buskirk?"

"Claudine made them. It's never too late to improve your diet." The old lady dabbed at her lips with a checkered napkin. "Nor too early. Eat up." And she guzzled the last of her tea.

"This is wonderful," Mark said.

"Yes," said Shannon. "You didn't have to do this, Mrs. van Buskirk."

"I enjoy it. It's nice to have company. So. Tell me about the relative that you're trying to find."

"We're looking for the grave of my father," Mark said.

"We'll just have a look at the map," Mrs. van Buskirk said.

Built into every nook and cranny of the kitchen were handsomely joined cupboards, slathered all over with generations of paint. The old lady addressed the lock of the tall narrow cupboard directly behind her, which yielded to a key she wore on a chain around her neck. The interior was much deeper than Mother Grey expected. Shelves lined the left wall, loaded with books, boxes, and tin files. Along the right wall were stored tall, flat items.

Mrs. van Buskirk put in her hand and slid out the official map of the Mount Outlook Cemetery Association, a huge yellowing chart mounted on pasteboard. "Mount Outlook Cemetery," said the superscription in an archaic typeface. It was marked off in a grid, coordinates A to Z across the top, 1 to 257 along the side. The plots were also marked grid-fashion, reminding Mother Grey of a map of Manhattan. Large sections of the cemetery were tinted different colors.

"The map looks old," Shannon said.

"It's a very old cemetery, dating from before the Civil War," Mrs. van Buskirk said. "Was your grandfather a veteran?"

"Yes," Mark said. "He served in France during World War II."

"Then the American Legion may have a record of where his grave is, if we aren't able to find it here. The

Legion puts flags on the graves of all the veterans every Memorial Day. What was his name?"

"James Smith. He died in 1955."

Squinting through a magnifying glass, she examined the map. Then she pulled out a small record book bound in blue-gray cloth and leafed through it, then a bigger book, brown with red corners. "Smith," she said, flipping through the pages of the larger book. "James Smith. Nineteen fifty-five, you say." Startled, she looked up. "Not Jimmy Smith?"

"I guess."

"I remember him. He was a wonderful man."

"Yes, he was."

"And so handsome." Mrs. van Buskirk looked again at Mark's face, a searching look this time. "You favor him a great deal," she said. "Of course when I knew him, he was younger." Her eyes glazed over, possibly with visions of the handsome man of yesteryear.

"Daddy, how old was your father when he died?"

"Thirty-two," Mark said.

"My word," said Mother Grey. *Scarcely out of adolescence.*

"The fact is, I'm a good deal older now than my father ever lived to be. The year I turned thirty-two, I had a bad time. I felt almost as though I wasn't supposed to get any older than my father, almost as though that was the age a man was supposed to live to be."

"It isn't very old at all," Delight van Buskirk said.

"As I've since come to see," said Mark. "Funny thing is, it was my wife who died that year."

Delight closed the ledger with a thump and let out a sigh. She took off her glasses and rubbed her eyes. "This is so hard to read."

The harp music had stopped, Mother Grey noticed with relief, how long ago she couldn't have said. She looked up to see the pale form of Claudine in the kitchen doorway, her arms crossed on her chest, her nasal adornment glittering in the kitchen lamplight, her other-worldly eyes boring into the back of Mark's head.

Mother Grey said, "Let me take a look, Mrs. van Buskirk. I might see something you missed."

Delight explained the grid system, where plots were identified by coordinates. Mother Grey looked at every name. There were Smiths, but no James W. Smith, and the Smiths she found were no relation, according to Delight, who knew everything about local bloodlines.

"It may be that he was buried with your mother's people," Delight suggested. "Her family name was Gilroy, wasn't it?"

"Fitzroy," Mark said. "Mary Agnes Fitzroy." No Fitzroy was to be seen, either in the ownership records or the records of burial. "But the Fitzroys were all Roman Catholics. They would have been buried in St. Joseph's graveyard," Mark said.

"Why isn't your father buried there?" Delight wondered.

"It seems strange, doesn't it?" Shannon said. "But Father de Spain says he's not." She hung over Mother Grey's shoulder and perused the map. "Look here. This part of the grid is on the access road, and yet the book says the whole Dismukes family is buried there."

"The map's not really current," Delight explained. "You must realize that the old cemetery fell on hard times for a while; the board has been working for the last five years to improve the records as well as the cemetery itself. Not all the access roads on the map really exist. I must say it's improved a great deal since I began to take an interest in it. And others in town, of course. Sometimes all a thing needs is a little attention."

"What happens to a cemetery when it falls on hard times?" Shannon asked.

"Vandalism. Things like that. And sometimes we have homeless people living in the mausoleums."

"My word," said Mother Grey.

"That won't be a problem anymore, though. We're having a welder come in and seal up the doors."

"What doors?" Mother Grey said.

"The doors to all those crypts. Weld them shut."

"My word. Are people still living in them?"

"Some vagrant or other." Delight van Buskirk dismissed the plight of this desperate poor person with a wave of her hand. Not that she herself was anything like rich; it was just that she and hers had worked hard all their lives, and she had no sympathy for those who didn't seem to want to. Mother Grey understood her feelings, though she didn't share them. Unlike Mother Grey, Mrs. van Buskirk had seen these people grow up, the dysfunctionals who made their homes in abandoned cars and makeshift shelters in the hills around Fishersville. Their names, ways, and early lives were known to her. Her own children had gone to school with some of them, in the days when they had homes, and she had discouraged her daughters from dating the boys. Time, she said, had vindicated her judgment. As for Christian charity, that was something one extended to strangers.

So Delight probably knew the cemetery squatter. "Would this vagrant be anyone I know?" Mother Grey asked. A procession of faces passed before her mind's eye—the hopeless, the drunkards, the disturbed Vietnam

vets who turned up from time to time at St. Bede's looking for help. It would not surprise her to hear of any one
of them living in a crypt in the cemetery.

Delight pursed her lips. "I would hope not," she said,
and about the so-called vagrant she would say no more.
She took up one of the record books and ran a knobby
finger down the pages, one after the other. "Here's a little
plot owned by the Rabsons. They were James's mother's
family. Phyllis Rabson Winkle would have been your
great-great-grandmother."

"Any record of anyone being buried on it?"

"Yes, indeed. Perrine Rabson and his two wives. Also
Phyllis Rabson Winkle and Horatio Winkle, and Ernes-
tine, your great-grandmother's sister who died when she
was a baby. And there are two empty plots, if either of
you ever wants to come here and be buried. To the best
of my knowledge, you're the last of the Rabsons."

Mark cleared his throat. "But no James W. Smith."

"No. Not buried, at least. It's coming back to me,
though. I seem to remember them putting up a memorial stone of some sort. They never found his body, did
they?"

"His body was missing?" Mark seemed surprised.

"Oh, no," Shannon said softly. "Whatever will we do
with Nana?" She took out the box of ashes and put it on
the kitchen table, as though to ask its advice.

Delight bridled. "What's that?"

"Nana's ashes. Actually we came here to Fishersville
to bury them next to my grandfather."

The old lady drew in her breath and let it out with a
shudder. "I do hope you weren't planning to do that
yourselves," she said.

"Shouldn't be much of a problem," Mark said.

"But you can't."

"We can't?" Shannon said.

"There are rules in the association. You can't just stick a box of ashes in the ground. Never mind that now, though. We'll sort it out after we find out about your grandfather." She returned to her record books, settling her glasses down on the end of her nose and paging furiously.

Claudine glided over to the table, stretched out her hand with its long painted nails, and laid it on the box. She closed her eyes. Everyone stared at her.

"Why did you bring her ashes back here?" she said at last.

"To bury her next to the spouse of her youth," said Shannon. "She never really had any other serious relationships. Not in forty years."

"You shouldn't have done it," Claudine whispered. "She left Fishersville to get away from him."

"To get away from who?" Mark said.

"That can't be true," said Shannon. "She would have told me. She told me everything."

Claudine seemed, if possible, even paler than usual, and for an instant Mother Grey thought she saw the girl's eyes begin to roll up in her head. "Are you all right?" she asked her.

Claudine blinked and looked around. "Fine," she said. "What is it? Did I say something?"

Delight squirmed with embarrassment. "She does things like this from time to time," she said. "It doesn't usually amount to anything."

"Well, thank you for your hospitality," Mark said. He stood up. "We really have to be going."

Shannon put the box back in the tote bag. "What's

the next step, do you think?" she said. "Someone must know how I can find my grandfather."

Claudine laid a hand on her arm. "I know this man at the New Age Center who does readings," she said. "He can probably tell you where your grandfather is. He'll need to know his birth date."

"Readings?"

"It's like he finds lost things. He has psychic powers."

"My word," Mother Grey said. A nervous laugh bubbled to her lips. Raving paganism, loose in Fishersville.

Claudine shot Mother Grey a hostile look and said to Shannon, "Call me later." She pressed a slip of paper into Shannon's hand.

Proselytizing for psychics. Today it's oat bran muffins, tomorrow Hinayana Buddhism or worse. Mother Grey had a sudden vision of Claudine leading Delight van Buskirk away from St. Bede's and off on some wacky spiritual journey through the New Age Center, stuffing her with herbs, festooning her with mystic beads, tying her ancient body up in yoga knots. It was too horrible to contemplate.

When she got home, Mother Grey fed and petted the animals and then looked at her answering machine.

The light was blinking.

Dave Dogg's voice, which she had not heard in three long months, spoke to her out of the black box: "It's me, Vinnie. Call me. I need to talk to you."

Dave Dogg. Calling from home, not the Trenton Police Station, where he worked as a homicide detective. They used to be—what?—sweethearts. The sound of his voice still caused her pulse to race. In those days he had wanted to marry her, had wanted her to make a place for him in her life. But her life belonged to the Church.

Then after a while she thought, well, maybe, but about that time his ex-wife Felicia came back.

She dialed his number; of course she still knew it by heart. But nobody answered.

3

"There's the New Age Center," Shannon said. Mark observed it sourly, caught in Bridge Street traffic on the way back to the hotel. It didn't look new; it looked about a hundred years old, a tall brick building. The morning sun poked through the clouds and glinted off the windows. "Why don't we park the car and go for a walk?" Shannon said. "I really want to see the town."

Mark did not want to see the town. Walk? Even rolling down the windows, smelling the rain on the pavement, made him uncomfortable. Why had he come here? When could he leave? Something terrible had happened here. Something terrible could happen again.

"You're awfully quiet," said Shannon.

"There was a big tree in front of that place," Mark said.

"Maybe it was an elm. They say the elm trees all died."

The old house. Again he remembered the face-powder smell, the hair brushing him.

Markie, get up, the water is coming.

He brushed the memory away, turned into the hotel parking lot.

"Come on," Shannon said. "Just walk around the block with me."

Strange things filled the store windows, imported garments, antiques. Shannon walked slowly, admiring a marble angel, then stopped to look at snapshots of properties for sale in the window of the local real estate agency.

"Look at these charming houses," said Shannon. "All for sale. Wouldn't it be fun to move here and live in one of these little places?"

Mark thought he recognized the house in the third photo from the left. It was the place where he and his family used to live. "That's our old house," he said. "I think."

"Really? You lived there?"

He pointed to the photo. "That was my room, and my parents slept there on the top floor. If that's the house. To think it should come on the market right when I'm in town."

Inside, a woman got up from the desk—they could see her through the window, between the taped pictures of property—and came to the front door of the office. "Are you interested in seeing a house?" she said.

"Yes," said Shannon; "No," said Mark. "This one," Shannon said, pointing to the photograph of the house with the porch.

The agent said, "I can show you that place right now; it's just around the corner. Let me lock up the office. That's a great place; it's right in the CBD."

"What's a CBD?" Shannon asked.

"Central business district. It's a zoning term. In the CBD you can rent to an antique dealer, or open a store. Your options are almost unlimited."

"But you could still have your residence in the CBD, couldn't you?" Shannon's eyes were shining. "We could move here, Daddy. You run your software business from home. This would do as well as our garage in Phoenix."

"Seems unlikely. I don't like it here." The more he saw and smelled and felt in Fishersville, the greater grew his sense of dread. "There's nothing here for me."

"If you want to live here," the agent said, "I can show you a place on North Union Street you'll really love."

"I want to see this one," Shannon said. "My dad lived there when he was little."

"Imagine that," the agent said.

The house was scarcely a block away. Mark still wasn't sure it was his family's old home. It was built on a corner on a sloping lot, more than a hundred feet deep, large for Fishersville. From the front two stories and an attic were visible. The front porch on the first story had a door in the center and a long window on each side. Had his mother looked out of this window at him, long ago, watching him play? Had his father?

The agent led them toward the back door. Mark followed behind her, and Shannon trailed after. He was thinking the yard smelled wrong, unfamiliar smells of mold, rotted vegetation, fried onions from the restaurant down the street. *This can't have been our house.*

"How high was the water here in 1955?" Shannon wondered. "This is the low end of town, right?"

"That was before my time," the agent said. "But I've seen pictures, and I guess it would be over our heads right here."

"Jeepers," Shannon said.

"It's not as though it will ever flood like that again," the agent said.

"What makes you think it won't?" Mark said.

"I don't know. These are modern times. People have things under control." She frowned, groping for the right word. "Technology," she said at last, beaming.

"Right, Daddy," Shannon said. "The fifties were the olden days, after all."

"The Mississippi still floods," Mark pointed out.

"Yes, but that's the Mississippi." The agent let them in.

The smell of the place—mold, rats, kerosene—was like a blow in the face. The smell of squalor, the smell of the past.

"This could be a really nice investment property," the agent said. She turned on the light, a pale bulb that hung from the ceiling. The floors were made of wide pine planks, a foot and a half to two feet. "See the pumpkin pine floors."

Mark hadn't realized how old this house must be. Pine trees in New Jersey hadn't reached a width of two feet in a hundred and fifty years.

"Right now they're using this room for a kitchen, but it has great possibilities," the agent said. He viewed the appointments of the kitchen: two tiny cabinets, a miniature sink, and a propane stove made to be used in a trailer. But why was he even thinking this way? He had no intention of buying this house.

"You could take out this partition and put in a whole new kitchen," the agent said. "If you wanted to use it for a residence. Or put the kitchen upstairs."

"Twenty-five thousand dollars right there," Mark responded automatically. This wasn't the old kitchen anyway. The real kitchen had been someplace else in the building. He saw his mother, suddenly, standing in the kitchen in a flowered housedress with her beautiful dark hair. A feeling of dread seized him. *Something had happened here.*

In an effort to bring himself back to the present, Mark put his hand on the old wallpaper and pushed gently. The wallpaper, the little flowers and background alike faded to muddy brown, felt solid and sound enough. No crumbling plaster underneath, but vertical black stains were showing along the wallpaper seams, soot seeping up from a malfunctioning furnace. He imagined moving in, scraping wallpaper, replacing the furnace. Impossible. Anyway, the house was haunted.

The agent opened a door to a room smaller than Mark's clothes closet back in Phoenix. Wedged between the walls was a toilet with a narrow tank. A tight fit. How would a fat person even sit down there?

There wasn't a basin.

"Show us the next floor," Shannon said. The next floor was the street level in the front of the house.

A narrow staircase led up between close walls, pressing in. How thin his parents must have been to live in such a place.

"This is the only staircase?" Shannon said.

"Right."

"I was thinking maybe these were the back stairs."

"No," said the agent.

Mark began to notice water damage: rotting plaster and long stains streaking down from the cracked ceiling to the warped floor. "Looks as though the roof leaks," he said.

"Oh, no, the roof is good and sound," the agent said. "Actually I believe that's from the upstairs bathroom."

"A center hall," Shannon said. "Nice."

"Yes," the agent said.

In that center hall the nails at the ends of the floorboards had come loose from the joists; the much-praised pumpkin pine wobbled and rocked under Mark's feet.

Water damage, deep and structural. Probably rot and termites as well. Just to the right of the center of his field of vision, flashing and glimmering, he became aware of a small hole, the first sign of an oncoming migraine attack.

What was he doing in this place?

The doorways of the two rooms on this level faced each other. Low ceilings, long and narrow rooms.

"Look at this nice mantel! There used to be a fireplace here," Shannon said. "And one in this room too." The fireplaces had been plastered over.

"You could open them up again," the agent said. "If you got somebody to look at the chimney."

The degree of neglect here, the depth of decay, was pressing on Mark like a weight. His head hurt.

The stairway to the next floor had a hardwood railing, old, polished, nicely turned, perhaps original with the house. He put his hand on it, felt the cool wood, and almost remembered everything. The post had been bigger then, taller than he was. As though in a dream he went up the creaking stairs to the next level.

In his old room other children had written names on the wall in the course of the last forty years. How small it was. But this wasn't where it had happened.

Markie, get up. The water is coming.

It had happened upstairs.

With a sensation that everything around him was shrinking, Mark started up the narrow, narrow stairway.

The bloodstain was still there.

Mother Grey and Towser were returning from a brisk run along the canal bank, making their way back along Bridge Street, when they nearly collided with Shannon Smith. She popped out of the door to the hotel just as they were passing.

"Mother Grey! I need to talk to you. Do you have a minute?"

"I suppose so. Where's your dad?"

"Lying down at the hotel. He's sick again."

"Again?"

"He gets these headaches all the time. Every couple of weeks," Shannon said. "His migraine will probably go away by this afternoon, but whether he'll be all right—I mean, really all right—I'm starting to wonder."

"What do you think is wrong?" They walked along together, heading toward the rectory.

"My dad hasn't been himself ever since Nana died. It's almost as though he's haunted."

"The process of grieving takes a long time."

"He leans on me. I feel as though I'm carrying him."

"Perhaps the two of you would benefit from counseling, or a support group. Did you look into that, when you were back home in Phoenix?"

"I thought maybe this trip would bring him some kind of closure," Shannon said. "But instead of that, he's just getting crazier. I mean haunted, literally haunted."

He has a ghost? "What do you mean?"

"Spirits haunt places because they're stuck there, right? They have to be released. My father is like that, stuck in some past event. He needs help to be released."

"You mean he himself is haunted?"

"He haunts himself." Shannon walked along with her head down, absorbed in thought. Then she turned suddenly to Mother Grey and held her gaze. "Can't you help him? Perform an exorcism or something?"

"What is it exactly that you want me to do?"

"Release my father from the ghost of himself, so that he can get on with his life, and I can get on with mine."

Perform an exorcism? What an idea. A picture flashed in Mother Grey's mind of the dignified Mark Smith being exorcised, his head spinning on his neck, cursing and spitting pea soup. "I think the effect you want can only be achieved through psychological counseling," she said. "Possibly even psychoanalysis. Months, even years of hard work on your father's part. I can't fix him by reciting a few words over him. I will pray for him, of course."

"I don't know what to do for him," the young girl whispered. Mother Grey noticed then that she was still carrying around the bookstore tote bag with its bulging box of ashes, and she thought, *Haunted, indeed. Your dad isn't the only one.*

"What are you going to do with your grandmother's ashes?"

"I don't know that either." They reached the front steps of the rectory. Shannon balanced the tote bag on the porch railing and looked at it as though it might speak to her. "If only I could find out what happened to my grandfather."

Mother Grey let the dog inside and took him off his leash. "It might help you to talk to people who knew your grandparents, or people who were here during the flood. Some of them are probably still in town."

"That might be the key to my dad's problems as well. If he could remember, or if someone could tell him what happened."

It was getting on past Mother Grey's lunchtime. Her stomach rumbled. "Have you had lunch?"

"Not yet."

"Why don't you come with me to Delio's luncheonette? A lot of the oldsters go there to eat; we can ask them what they remember about the flood and about your grandfather."

"Do you think they would know?"

"It can't hurt to ask."

"Wouldn't it be great if I could have the whole mystery unraveled before Dad even woke up? He could find peace of mind at last, and we could go back to Phoenix. He wants to do that."

"Yes. It would be great." Mother Grey pictured Mark Smith's face, the angry, puzzled face of a troubled child. His father's death had scarred him in ways still visible after forty years. The death of his mother, Nana of the ashes, had wounded him afresh. That he could become unhaunted in a single afternoon seemed unlikely.

But picking up a piece or two of the puzzle was a job she could undertake. That was doable.

Mark Smith's father, then. Who was he? What happened to him in 1955?

4

The stroll to Delio's took them past a long row of antique stores. "Look at that angel," Shannon said, stopping in front of a display of a stone statue with feathery wings outspread. "Did you ever see anything so lovely? I'd like to have it in my garden, if I had a garden."

"I think it belongs in a cemetery," Mother Grey said. She often saw artifacts in the antique store windows of Fishersville that had clearly come from churches or graveyards, but she usually passed by them without feelings of outrage because they were on the periphery of her vision, like cockroaches in a dark kitchen. You could ignore them if you didn't look straight at them. But if you did look—"I think it came from a cemetery, in fact," she was forced to observe.

"How romantic! Pillaged two hundred years ago by brigands."

"More likely pillaged the day before yesterday by people from Cleveland. Here's the luncheonette."

They were a bit early for lunch, and Delio's was empty of customers. Proprietor Lou de Leo was shredding lettuce against the imminent demand for hoagies. Mother Grey and Shannon ordered ham sandwiches and selected a table while he put them together.

Seeing how Shannon clutched the tote bag against her chest, Mother Grey was moved to wonder about the woman whose ashes it contained. "Tell me about Mary Agnes," she said. "What was she like?"

Shannon put the bag down and stared off into space. "She raised me. She was a mother to me. She was tough—she had to be tough to survive everything she went through, a single parent, making a whole new life for herself in the West, and then the breast cancer."

"My word. She had breast cancer?"

"In 1956. I guess they didn't do chemotherapy in those days; she said the doctors put her to sleep for a biopsy, and when she woke up, they had done a radical mastectomy on her, cutting the muscle and everything."

"But it saved her life."

"Saved her life, yes. But it was so awful for her. I think in a way she never recovered. Still she could be a lot of fun sometimes. She used to tell me stories about the things she did in the old days, how they danced to the big bands, how all the boys wanted to marry her."

"Really!"

Lou brought them their sandwiches. "She had seven proposals," Shannon said, and took a bite.

"My word. Why did she choose your grandfather? Did she say?"

"He was handsome, he was witty, he was a good dancer. Mostly he was handsome. She almost didn't marry him. Just before he went away to war, he called up and wanted her to elope with him."

"And did she?"

"No. It's kind of a long story." And Shannon proceeded to tell it, how Jim Smith's favorite expression was "No future in it"—"Shall we see a movie tonight? Eat a hamburger?" "No future in it," he used to say—how when he called from Fort Dix one stormy night, saying he was shipping out and could she run away and marry him first, "No future in it" was the first answer that popped into her head. In the middle of a terrific storm, the telephone had rung: "Darling, I'm shipping out," he'd said. "Let's drive to Elkton tonight and get married."

Her father wouldn't let her take the car.

Or she wouldn't let herself take the car. She was looking at a terrible ordeal for nothing but love, and she said, "I can't." Forty miles of bad road lay between them; in her imagination she could hear the crack of pine trees snapping off in the storm, falling across the narrow track to Fort Dix, could see the floods rising up over the road to Maryland.

"I can't," she said, "there's no future in it." He argued with her, so she tried to mollify him. "When you get back, we'll be married in the church, the way people are supposed to be, in front of Father John, with my mother and father and everybody there. I'll write to you every day." She did write to him every day, and when he came back to Fishersville, still alive at the end of the war, they were married in the church sure enough.

"She said there was a boy who stayed behind who was terribly in love with her; the army wouldn't take him because he was lame or something. But she wouldn't have him because she was waiting for my grandfather. Jim Smith was her fate."

"She told you the whole story," Mother Grey marveled.

"It was like a movie. She was always telling me stories, her own and her girlfriends', thrilling tales of romance and lost love, because she knew I wanted to be a writer."

"Really," said Mother Grey. "What sort of thing do you write?"

"Fiction. Someday I'll write a book."

"The great American novel."

"Why not? It's out there waiting to be written."

"But you know, I find myself wondering," Mother Grey said. "Did your grandmother believe a writer should have a different understanding of life from any other person's?"

"What do you mean?"

"If she thought you meant to be, say, a plumber, would she have kept these stories to herself, do you suppose?"

"She might have," Shannon said. "Except that she enjoyed telling them. I agree with her that it's important for a writer to know how people feel. Like, I've never been seriously in love. But it's something you have to write about. Tell me something, Mother Grey. Do you believe in love at first sight? I saw this man yesterday at the cemetery, standing in the rain—"

"Love at first sight can be risky," said Mother Grey, thinking of her own amatory troubles. Had she fallen for

Dave at first sight? No, but she had noticed him, and things had developed from there. Things had developed, and then deteriorated again. It was he who claimed to have fallen in love at first sight. But that was then. Fortunately she had managed to banish all thoughts of the feckless Dave Dogg from her mind and heart, and very successfully. She never thought of him. As for why he might have called her on the phone yesterday afternoon, out of a clear blue sky, she was scarcely even curious. "Speaking for myself," she said, "I detest romantic pain, although it's diverting in books sometimes. If I had a daughter, I would teach her to try to avoid it."

"She told me lots of things besides the stories of romantic pain. She told me about old times in Fishersville. It was kind of a golden age for her, when life was interesting and real. Sometimes I felt as though she were trying to send me back here."

"How do you mean?"

"It was, like, she couldn't come back, but I was supposed to come back and do something she hadn't done."

"I don't get it. Did she say what?"

"No." Shannon put her sandwich down and wiped a bit of mustard off her lips. "And now it's too late to do anything except bury her. Although Claudine says . . ." Her voice trailed off, her gaze shifted.

Claudine has told her not to tell me anything they talked about. Strange, subtle girl. What was she up to?

"Did Claudine say any more to you about her idea that your grandmother ran away from Fishersville to get away from your grandfather?"

"It was just a feeling she had," Shannon said. "Craziness. I don't see why Nana would tell Claudine anything after she was dead that she wouldn't tell me when she was alive. We were very close."

"But you believe she wanted you to come back here."

"She did want me to come back here. Or to go back into the past for her. I don't know. I thought I'd figure it out when we got here, but all we did was go up to the graveyard, and then it was like everyone was dead. I kept stumbling across the graves of people Nana used to get Christmas cards from." Mother Grey thought Shannon was going to start crying again.

"Your grandmother would be surprised at the changes here since 1955," she said, hoping to lead her thoughts to something less depressing.

It worked; the girl brightened up. "It's not so different, you know. I took a walk around town last night after the rain stopped, and I thought in a way Fishersville hasn't changed that much. In a way it's all still here."

"You're right," Mother Grey said. "The Acme, the cemetery—oh, well, they closed the Acme a few months ago, but the building is still standing. Speaking of the fifties—now there's a real period piece."

"We don't have anything like it in Phoenix. And those tiny little houses built so close together. Do the people still sit out on their porches in warm evenings with the lights off?"

"Yes," Mother Grey said. You could still walk down Buttonwood Street on a summer night saying *Hi, H'lo,* and voices would answer softly out of the dark, *Howya doin'.*

"Everybody used to go to church on Sunday morning," Shannon said.

"Lots of people still do that," Mother Grey said. *Not to my church, of course, but this will change.*

"They're all in the cemetery now, the girls she played bridge with, the boys who wanted to marry her. She used to get letters and Christmas cards from them. She used to tell me their life stories."

"But she never came back to see them."

"It's sad. I remember all their names. Mabel Weeds was a good friend of hers. Do you know if she's still alive?"

"I don't know a Mabel Weeds," Mother Grey said. "But there are lots of folks in town I don't know." If she wasn't a parishioner, a city official, a homeless person, a regular at St. Bede's AA, or a member of the clergy, chances were Mother Grey wouldn't know her by name, though there were many in town whose faces she knew.

Here came three of them now, the ladies who always took the corner table by the window, wearing baseball caps and pastel running suits. They smiled and waved; they knew Mother Grey, probably by name. Why not? In the past seven years she had become one of the town characters.

The old lady in aqua looked again at Shannon, and then whispered to the others. They all stared at the girl, muttering. Then the first one got up and came over to their table.

"I don't mean to intrude, but you look so like someone I once knew. I'm Mabel Weeds."

"Mrs. Weeds! I'm so happy to see you! I'm Shannon Smith." She gave the old lady an impulsive hug.

"Shannon is Mary Agnes's granddaughter," Mother Grey said.

"Of course," said Mrs. Weeds, her eyes devouring the girl's face. "It's been so long since I heard from Mary Agnes. How is she?"

"She died in February, actually," Shannon said.

"Oh." Old people are never really surprised to hear of the death of one of their number, but still they hate it. "Was she sick long?" Mrs. Weeds asked.

"No, it was very sudden. Her heart."

"It's Mary Agnes's granddaughter!" she called to the others. They got up and came over, admiring her.

"The picture of Mary Agnes," one of them said. "Who was it she married?"

"That boy Jim Smith, when he came back from the war in Europe."

"Was that Jim Smith who was the foreman in the umbrella factory, or Jim Smith the police chief?"

"Neither. It was the Jim Smith who traveled around selling construction equipment."

"Oh. Him. He died, didn't he?"

"Yes, he's dead. They made such a handsome couple. Didn't they have a child?"

"My father," Shannon said.

"Oh, right. Of course."

"This is Shannon's first visit to Fishersville," Mother Grey said. "She wants to know about the old days. She wants to hear stories about the great flood."

"Come and sit with us," said Mrs. Weeds. "We'll tell you all about it." They pushed another table up against their corner table.

"It was a lot of water," said the old lady in pink. "On our street they came and got people out of their houses in a boat."

"I was here then," said the one in blue. "But I don't remember much. I wasn't old enough. It was scary, though. I remember that. I kept asking my mother if the water would come up to our house, and she said it wouldn't, and sure enough it didn't. Just the same we had to get typhoid shots, and drinking water from the Red Cross. The waterworks was flooded, and the water was no good for a long time."

As the women told their flood stories, other regulars drifted in, ordering lunch, finding seats at the tables or the counter. Mother Grey felt a stab of guilt at the sight of Peter Susswald, the bookstore owner; she had failed to return his invitation to the quarterly cemetery party of the Friends of Mount Outlook, in which they were to do cleanup and recording chores to help maintain the old graveyard. It was tomorrow. As Peter bellied up to the counter to order his lunch, she tried to remember whether she had meant to decline or accept. The parties were always fun. Peter had adopted the cemetery as his favorite local project shortly after he came to town to open his secondhand bookstore. It was he who founded the Friends of Mount Outlook, though no relatives of his were buried there. Like Mother Grey, the former college professor was an outsider.

The other folks swarming in to get their lunches were old-time locals: Horace Burkhardt, the old man who lived next door to Mother Grey, and his crony Archie Vogel; Matt Pollard and his roofing crew; Wally Pascoe. Everyone took an interest in the flood stories. "August 18, 1955." said Pollard, a faraway smile glazing his features. "Hurricane Diane. I remember it well."

"We had martial law, I remember that," said an oldster at the end of the counter. "The National Guard had to come to stop the looting."

"I don't know about any looting," another man said. "But I had to spend that whole weekend helping dig out the Acme. They had to throw away tons of food; it was all contaminated." After the flood waters went down, he said, the damage to the back part of the Acme was so extensive that they had to replace part of the concrete floor.

"Ferryman did that work, didn't he?" Matt Pollard said.

"You mean John Ferryman who lives up by the cemetery, or George Ferryman who died?"

"John."

"John. Yeah. He did that work."

"Shame about his son." A moment of silence. Mother Grey understood from what was not being said that they all knew some disagreeable piece of gossip about Ferryman's son, whoever he might be. She resolved to track it down later. As a figure in the community, she felt that she had a duty to keep on top of things.

Archie Vogel dug his elbow into Horace's ribs. "Remember that big old fish we found flopping around?"

"Yeah, it swam into the store and it couldn't swim out. What was that, a shad?"

"Naw, it was a big trout."

One of the women sighed. "They had to close the Acme because of all the damage. You couldn't get any food, and then when you could, there wasn't any power to cook it. We had to go to the Baptist church, where the Red Cross was feeding people."

"How brave you all must have been to stay here after such a disaster," Shannon said.

"No reason to leave. This is the greatest place in the world," Archie Vogel said, "and I've seen some places."

"I agree," Peter Susswald said. Lou de Leo (born and raised in Fishersville but too young to have seen the flood) gave Susswald his lunch, wrapped to go, and he paid for it. At last he caught Mother Grey's eye. "Are you coming to the work party tomorrow?"

"Yes," she said. Or was there somewhere else she was supposed to be? How tiresome, she didn't have her calendar with her. If only she could remember to keep up with her correspondence.

"Great," he said. "We're having the usual wine and cheese. If you want to know about the flood," he added as he headed for the door, "you ought to go look at the Acme. They say there's still a high-water mark in the back storeroom. See you."

"You'd better look quick," said Matt Pollard. "They're going to start the remodeling tomorrow."

"What! On a Saturday?" Archie Vogel cried.

"It's the only time they could get the power shovel."

Matt Pollard squinted at Shannon. "Did somebody say you were related to Jim Smith?"

"Did you know my grandfather?" Shannon asked.

"I went to school with him," Pollard said.

"What was he like?" Shannon asked.

"Greatest guy in the world," Pollard said.

"That's what they say," Mrs. Weeds agreed. "Sports hero, war hero, all the girls were in love with him, and all the men admired and looked up to him. When he and Mary Agnes were finally married, the other girls were crushed, and the other men were crushed too, because they were all in love with Mary Agnes."

"I remember the day they were married," another woman said. "We gathered all the flowers of May from our gardens and brought them to the church. They were so much in love."

"I remember the day he died," Matt Pollard said. "Tragic."

"Do you remember how it happened?" Shannon asked.

"The flood got him. It was about four in the morning. The water was coming up fast. Awful noises, trees and pieces of houses crashing against the bridge supports. He took a boat and went to rescue a couple stranded on their roof. The Widsons, wasn't it?"

"They're dead too?"

"That's right. She died just last year." It seemed to Mother Grey that the old folks punctuated most of their remarks with murmurs about the departed. "He's dead, isn't he?" "Yeah, dead." "He's dead." "Mmm-hmm, dead."

"But they had to be rescued by someone else, because Jim couldn't get to them. The boat was swept into the current somehow, and he was never seen again."

"Jeepers," Shannon said.

"Nor the boat either," Archie Vogel muttered darkly.

"That was how he died?" Shannon said.

"Yes, dear," the little old lady said. "Your granddad was a big hero."

"We never knew for certain," Shannon said. "My father was so young when it happened, and it upset Nana so much that she wouldn't talk about it at all."

Matt Pollard said, "Remember the day they dedicated that memorial to him up on Mount Outlook?"

"Nobody was there but his mother and father and the boat club members. Mary Agnes had left town by then," Archie Vogel said.

Mabel Weeds sighed. "She never came back, not even to dedicate his memorial stone."

"Father John wouldn't come and bless it either. He wouldn't even let them put it in the Smith plot in St. Joseph's graveyard," Archie said.

"Why was that?" Shannon asked.

"Ask Father John," Archie muttered darkly.

"Can't, he's dead."

"Dead. Him too."

"Right."

"Where is that memorial? We weren't able to find it," Shannon said.

"It's in the Rabson plot on Mount Outlook. Rabsons were your great-grandfather's mother's people," Mrs. Weeds said to Shannon.

"Go on up and see it. It's a pretty thing, has a ship carved on it," Matt Pollard said.

"Is it still there?" one of the men asked.

"Where would it go?"

"No place, only I ain't seen it lately."

Archie Vogel wagged his shaggy eyebrows. He had a secret, he seemed to be saying, and it wouldn't be a secret for long. "Didn't you ever wonder why Father John wouldn't let them put the monument in St. Joseph's cemetery?"

"No, Archie. Why was that?"

"Father John knew he killed himself on purpose."

"Archie, that's enough," Mrs. Weeds said. "You shouldn't say such things in front of the man's granddaughter."

"Do you happen to know what gave Father John such an idea?" Shannon asked.

"He seen him do it."

"Oh."

"Father John was out there in the middle of the night helping flood victims. So he looked out on the river, and there went Jimmy amongst all them floating trees and houses, standing up in a rowboat. Next thing he knew he steered right for the wing dam, and over he went. On purpose."

"That can't be true," said Mrs. Weeds. "How in the world could Father John have seen him way out on the river in the middle of the night?"

"I guess he saw him get in the boat, and then he watched him row out and go over the falls."

"You're making this up."

"Then you tell me why Jim Smith's memorial stone was put up in the Mount Outlook Cemetery and not in St. Joseph's."

"Because his mother's people owned a plot there," Mrs. Weeds said very reasonably.

"Nope. It was because of Father John." The old man drank the last of his coffee and banged the cup down in the saucer. "I know what I know." He drew his sleeve across his mouth.

Matt Pollard didn't like his story. "Jim Smith had no reason to kill himself, Archie. From what I understand, he had a business, a family, good friends. Why would he kill himself? It doesn't make sense."

"I know what I know, I tell you."

"Jim Smith was a war hero. He wasn't the kind of man who would take the coward's way out," Horace said.

"Out of what?" Mother Grey wondered aloud, before she could stop herself.

"He had plenty of reason to kill himself," Archie said. "Mary Agnes was in love with another man."

"Oh, yes. You, I suppose," Mrs. Weeds said.

"No, we all know who."

"That's as much motive for someone else to kill him as it is for him to kill himself," Horace said. "This other man, for instance. Who might he have been? Speak up. We're all listening."

And they all were. Was the other man present among these old folks? But Archie sank his head back down between his shoulders, turtlelike, and mumbled again that he knew what he knew.

Mrs. Weeds wasn't going to let it go that easily. "Tell me this, then, Archie," she said. "What makes you hate him so?"

A long silence. Finally he spoke: "It was my goddamned boat he stole."

With various exclamations and grunts of disgust, the others crumpled their sandwich wrappers, slurped the last of their drinks, and readied their plastic plates for the trash. Lunch was over; it was time to move on. In moments the luncheonette was empty except for the three old ladies, Shannon, and Mother Grey.

The reported sighting of the memorial stone, the one with the ship, was encouraging. "Do you think your father has recovered from his headache?" Mother Grey asked. "We should try the cemetery again, now that the weather is clear and we know where to look."

"Not yet," Shannon said. "Dad won't be ready to face the world for another hour or two. Let's you and me go check out the Acme. Then I'll go get Dad and meet you at the cemetery to see this memorial stone." She patted the tote bag. "With any luck we'll be all ready to leave town tonight." They settled with Lou de Leo for the lunch check and went outside, where Shannon stopped and stood still for a moment on the sidewalk.

"Did you notice how they all told different stories about my grandfather's death?" she said.

"That isn't unusual," Mother Grey said. "More than

forty years have passed, after all. Even with something that happened the day before yesterday, witnesses generally don't remember things the same way."

"They all told completely different stories. Do you think there was something strange about the way my grandfather died?"

"Oh, yes," Mother Grey said. "Clearly. But if we keep digging, we can find out what really happened. I'm sure it will turn out to be perfectly . . ." What? Wholesome? Normal? It was the fifties, after all, when everything was wholesome and normal, even sudden death.

Mrs. Weeds looked out the door of the luncheonette and beckoned to them. Her friends were still inside, preoccupied with paying. "Come and see me this afternoon," she whispered. "Both of you. I have something to show you." She gave Mother Grey her address, scribbled on the back of a napkin, and ducked inside again.

Several months had passed since the sad day when the Acme closed up. As stylish as the old supermarket had been, in its retro way, as easy to get to for those who liked to shop on foot, the Acme had failed to do the volume of business required by the front office in Philadelphia or wherever it was. Now the old Acme building, with its tower and its cream-and-blue exterior, stood empty. If the locals were to be believed, it would come down tomorrow or at best be renovated out of all possible recognition. Turned into another antique store, was the word on the street, although the *Clarion* kept running stories of how Mayor Joe Budge had nailed down a promise from some food-store chain or other to move in and open up.

A large muddy pickup truck was parked in the Acme lot. In the back of it were ladders, shovels, a built-in toolbox, a wheelbarrow, and a small concrete mixer. It was red with black lettering that read: "John Ferryman, Fishersville, NJ." Ferryman, the mason who lived up by the cemetery and had the unfortunate son.

Mother Grey pressed her nose against the Acme's front window. Was anything going on in there? Without the lights, the checkout counters, the shelves, the food, and the back wall that used to block the public view of the butcher shop and storeroom, the old Acme was little more than a huge gray cave. Easy enough to imagine it full of water, or rats, or demons, or anything else.

"What do you see?" said Shannon.

"There's a man in there."

He was standing in a patch of light far in the back, hands on his hips, seemingly staring at the place where the wall met the floor; an older man in coveralls, solidly built, with a head of unruly white hair.

The door was open, propped with a bucket. They went in. "Hello," called Mother Grey. A hollow echo.

"Howya doin'," the man called back. "Help you with something?" He took a few steps toward them, walking with a slight limp.

"We came to see the high-water mark," Shannon said.

"From what? Last winter?"

"No, the flood of 'fifty-five," Mother Grey said.

"I can show you that. Come on back."

They picked their way across the worn and broken tiles, among screws and brackets where rows of shelves had once been secured to the floor. This used to be the chili and macaroni aisle. Mother Grey was seized with

53

nostalgia. Not that the food had been all that wonderful, but at least you could buy it without getting in your car and driving, and the staff all knew who you were.

"Here it is," said Shannon.

"Wouldn't be on that wall," said the man. "That wall is new since the flood."

"Are you sure?"

"Should be. I put it in myself. I think what you're looking for is over here." He look more closely at Shannon.

"Where?" she said.

"Who are you?" he said.

"Excuse me?"

"Sorry," he said. "You look like somebody, is all."

"You probably knew my grandmother. They say I look like her."

"Who's she?"

"Mary Agnes Smith. She died last February."

"Mary Agnes is dead?" It was a cry of anguish. The stricken man sank to a sitting position on the nearest thing, which was an old crate, and put his face in his hands. He was weeping.

"I'm sorry, I didn't mean to shock you this way," Shannon said. She put her arm around his shoulder while Mother Grey patted his hand, but he would not be comforted.

At length a wrinkled white handkerchief came out of his pocket. He blew his nose and sighed. "I always thought we would see each other one more time."

"You're John, aren't you?" Shannon said.

"She told you about me?"

"Of course."

5

For a long time Mark Smith lay facedown across the motel room bed, unable to move, waiting for the pain to go away. A towel, wrung out in cold water, lay across the back of his neck. When he began to shiver, he pulled the coverlet over himself and escaped into sleep.

When Mark had a migraine attack, the pain was only part of his trouble. His thought processes became thick. Even in dreams he had no power of concentration; unpleasant images appeared to him and vanished again before he could grasp their meaning.

Brown water, surging, gushing. Huge trees rushing toward his house, battering at the walls, crashing through the front windows. Branches reaching for him.

At the top of the stairs, the door banging open. His mother coming out.

Blood on her shoe.

He woke suddenly to the sound of Shannon's key in the lock and sat up. His head was swimming, but the pain was gone.

"How are you, Daddy?"

"All better. Where've you been?"

"Mother Grey and I went detecting. We found out a lot of things. Is it okay if I turn the light on?"

"Go ahead. What did you find out?"

"One of the old folks of the town says your dad died in an act of great heroism, trying to rescue a family from their rooftop."

"Really."

"Somebody else tried to tell me he stole his boat."

"He stole a boat?"

"Yes. Claims he saw him when he did it."

"It must have been someone wearing his clothes."

"Why would you think that?"

"I remember something," Mark said. Was it memory, or dreams?

"Something about the way he died?"

"In the house. There was blood. The stains are still there, by the way."

Shannon put the tote bag down. "Is that what made you sick today?"

"No, it was that stinking dinner we got at the restaurant last night."

"I liked it."

"You didn't order what I had."

"You know, Daddy, you ought to consider talking to somebody about things."

"Like who?"

"I don't know. A counselor. Maybe even a hypnotist.

Somebody who can help you drag all these dreams and feelings into the daylight, so they'll stop giving you headaches. Claudine van Buskirk knows somebody at the New Age Center."

"Honest, sport, it was the food." He got up and went into the bathroom. More cold towels, one on his face this time, cleared his head some.

"I found John," she called to him.

"John who?"

"Ferryman. Nana's old boyfriend."

"That's his story," Mark said.

"He still thinks about her. He cried when I told him she was dead."

"No kidding."

"I thought it was terribly romantic."

"Do I want to meet this person?" Mark said.

"Yes. You do. I think he's very nice."

Not so nice, Mark thought. John Ferryman. Low voices in the middle of the night, the smell of rye whiskey . . .

The night of the flood? Or some other night?

"Come with me," Shannon said. "Mother Grey and I figured out where to find Grandfather's memorial stone. If we hurry, we can find it while there's still some daylight. I told Mother Grey we'd meet her in the cemetery."

The melting snow of Mount Outlook Cemetery was crisscrossed with tracks—squirrel's tracks, cat's tracks, dog's tracks, bootprints, the marks of high heels, the spoor of a surprisingly large amount of traffic for a place where unauthorized entrance was supposed to be forbidden. Half visible behind tall stones and obelisks, people could be seen moving here and there despite the cyclone fence; one man held a squatting dog on a leash. Mother Grey quickened her pace, meaning to encourage him to pick up after his dog in accordance with local ordinances, but before she could draw within hailing distance, both dog and man ran away.

Drawn up on the shoulder of one of the access roads was a truck fitted with heavy lifting equipment—installing a headstone, probably. In the distance she could see flashes and hear the hiss and crackle of acetylene torches at work. *Minions of the cemetery association,* thought Mother Grey, *sealing up the doors to the tomb to keep out the needy.* There was useful Christian symbolism in that somewhere, though she couldn't quite put her finger on it. If the concept jelled by Sunday, she could use it in her sermon.

She sat down for a moment's rest. The first tiny pale-green leaves of spring were pushing out of their buds on trees and bushes. The whole cemetery lay to the east, peaceful and beautiful in the late afternoon sun. The careful rows of headstones curled over the curve of the hillside, some plain, some fancy; here and there a crypt burrowed into the hill, each with its ornate bronze door; at the summit stood the Wagonner mausoleum, a late Victorian brownstone, more solidly built than most of the houses in Fishersville, including St. Bede's rectory.

She rose and walked upward until she came to Hester Winkle's grave, freshly sodded and bedecked with flowers. She turned around to view the houses in the town below, clustered along the bank of the Delaware River, the canal threading beside it, and the old factories, none of them working anymore. A clear day. Across the river in Bucks County, she could see all the way to the

clock tower of the Sunnybrae Gardens retirement community, where poor Hester had spent her last years in
the cognitive impairment ward. *At rest at last,* she
thought, and said a prayer for the soul of the old lady.

Mother Grey was never made sad or apprehensive by
coming to this place, not like her visits to Hester in Sunnybrae. Death held no terrors for her, nor was Mount
Outlook a place where she herself would come to mourn,
for her own people—husband, parents, grandparents—
were buried on another hill in a village in Maryland.

In fact she regarded Mount Outlook as a park. It was
almost a shame that the cemetery association discouraged the living from frequenting it. The place where she
had been sitting was a great semicircular marble bench
. dedicated to the memory of a city merchant. As a bench
it was not uncomfortable, and the view was magnificent.
Yet nobody ever came up from the town to lounge there.

Perhaps it was the association's fault. *When cemeteries are outlawed,* she thought, *only outlaws will occupy
the cemeteries.* There went an outlaw now, no doubt, disappearing over the brow of the hill, a stranger in work
clothes and a scraggly beard. She caught a sudden whiff
of excrement, human this time, and it occurred to her
that Delight van Buskirk had a point after all; people
should not try to live in graveyards.

The Smiths were nowhere in sight. Nobody was,
now. She climbed a little higher and nearly stumbled
over the last live person in the cemetery, crouching over
a gravestone and making a strange hissing noise.

What on earth was he doing? Mother Grey cleared
her throat. "Hem-hem."

He turned and smiled at her. She found herself looking into the china-blue eyes of the handsomest man she

had ever seen in the flesh, movie-star handsome, with pale yellow hair, white teeth (whose slight irregularity added to their charm), an elegant jawline, and the kind of tan one develops through years of winter sports. A face of paralyzing good looks. Recovering herself, she said hello.

"Hello," he said.

"What are you doing?"

He stood up and wiped his hands on his thighs, tightly encased in well-aged blue jeans. She could now see that he had been smearing Barbasol on an old gravestone.

"I am engaged in genealogical research," he said. He put out his hand. "Dieter von Helden. How do you do— Reverend, is it?" She was wearing her clerical collar.

The handsome stranger was European, by his accent. The tourists were coming from farther and farther afield, creeping into ever more obscure corners of Fishersville. She had never encountered one in the cemetery, though. She took his hand; it was firm and muscular.

"How do you do," she said. "Lavinia Grey." It seemed odd to be shaking hands with a strange man in the middle of a cemetery, but he was completely at ease.

"Observe," he said, and returned to the tombstone to demonstrate his technique. By passing a sort of squeegee across the shaving cream, he caused the weather-worn inscription to become legible:

In Memory of Paul William Manford
January 1829 to April 1892
Husband and Father
"gone but not forgotten"

"Marvelous," she said. He took a picture of it. "Are you a professional genealogist, Mr. von Helden, or are you researching your own family?"

"Amateur only, Reverend Grey. Professionally I am an actor. My great-aunt is married to a man from Fishersville, and so I look in the graveyard here for his people. I am preparing a book of family history as a gift for their fiftieth wedding anniversary."

"What a nice gift."

He shrugged. "They seem to have everything else."

"But it's so much work," she said.

"Not with modern technology. This takes digital pictures"—he flourished the camera—"and I have a genealogical software product on this laptop computer"—he patted a black shoulder bag—"where I can organize everything."

The idea of carrying ancestors around in a shoulder bag reminded her of Shannon, with her grandmother in a shoebox. Where was that girl, anyway? "How does it work?"

"You enter the names, dates, and relationships, and it makes the charts and family trees. Later on I can print it out and bind it in a book for Aunt Kersten."

"Family research is not something I was ever moved to do," Mother Grey admitted.

"Well, of course not. For the Christian, all of us are brothers and sisters, isn't it so? Genealogy is irrelevant. Although the Mormons get very excited about it, I understand. For them, bloodlines have to do with salvation. They keep some of the best genealogical records in the United States, I promise you."

"I didn't know that."

"So you've never researched your ancestors?"

"No need to." Granny had known all about every-body—ancestors, cousins, the works—and she had writ-ten everything down. They used to look at her scrapbook with the old pictures every summer when they went to Mount Anna. The scrapbook was there still, no doubt, in the cottage that had gone to a cousin when Granny died. Anytime she wanted, she could drive to Maryland and see it.

And yet she never had. Well, that would be in another lifetime. Footsteps crunched on the access road behind her; she turned and saw the Smiths approaching.

"Hey! Over here!" said Dieter von Helden. He was waving at them. Shannon waved back.

"Do I know you?" said Mark, as they approached.

Shannon said, "You remember, Daddy, he was here yesterday during the rainstorm."

"I hope you found the grave you were looking for yesterday," von Helden said. His smile was radiant, like the sun coming out; Mother Grey could feel the warmth of it, and she could see that Shannon did as well.

"Not yet. What are you doing? When I saw you stand-ing in the rain, I thought you were grieving for some-one."

"No, no. I was making notes for a genealogy project. I am researching the family of the husband of my aunt." He went down on his knees again, in a graceful, athletic way, and rubbed off the shaving cream with a rag. Mother Grey and Shannon watched him, half-hoping he would give them another of those dazzling smiles, but Mark pulled them away.

"Not my idea of a useful activity," said Mark. "Ceme-teries are a waste of good acreage that could be used by the living. Come on, ladies. I think that memorial stone is farther up the hill."

"We should have made a copy of Delight's map," Mother Grey said, "or at least a sketch of where the Rabson plot is."

"It's this way," Shannon said. "About five plots north of the access road. I noticed the place on the map." They plodded onward, and then Mother Grey saw the angel, a prominent feature of the Rabsons' turf. Its outstretched hands blessed the graves of long-deceased Rabsons and their spouses, whose infants were planted in little short spaces between the head- and footstones. Shannon admired it, and then she noticed the dates on the tombstones and the little short spaces between the headstones and the footstones.

"Dead babies," she murmured.

"Cholera, diphtheria. The olden days were dangerous times," said Mother Grey.

"My great-grandfather's headstone," Mark said. "What's this stuff all over it?"

Mother Grey took a look. It was shaving cream. "I guess Herr von Helden has been here," she said. "Or maybe some other genealogist."

"But where is the memorial stone?" Shannon said.

"Keep looking," said Mark.

Shannon searched behind trees and under bushes, while Mark paced in a wide circle, examining the ground as though the elusive memorial stone might have sunk into the mud somehow. As they went over the ground for the third time, Mother Grey heard a man's voice calling her name.

"Mother Vinnie!" She looked up over the brow of the hill to see Wally Pascoe, one of the local workmen, standing beside the entrance to the Wagonner tomb. In his right hand he held an acetylene torch. "Can you come here a minute?"

Mother Grey approached the tomb and saw that its ornate bronze doors stood open. She was no stranger to this building; here she had read the burial service over her one-time friend and fellow musician, Phyllis Wagonner. In the old days when the umbrella factory was working, the Wagonners had been the town's leading industrialists. Now that the factory was closed and the last living Wagonner was far away, the palatial family vault looked sad and neglected; weeds grew all around.

"Mrs. van Buskirk says I'm supposed to weld these doors shut," Wally said. "She told me to take the stuff out and give anything useful to charity. I don't know nothin' about charity, but I thought maybe you could use it at St. Bede's, Mother Vinnie."

A sleeping bag, a camp stove, a tattered rucksack, and a litter of empty potato chip bags and soda bottles lay on the muddy tiled floor. The camping equipment was of fairly good quality. "I suppose so," Mother Grey said, and dragged out the sleeping bag and the camp stove. At a minimum she could get it back into the hands of the homeless person who owned it. "What a mess. Have you got a broom, before you seal this up?" He did, and as the two of them cleaned out the inside of the mausoleum, Mother Grey had time once again to admire the stained glass window, a representation of funereal lilies, and the blue-and-white patterned mosaic tile of the floor. Behind the north wall rested the mortal remains of Phyllis. An empty space above waited for Phyllis's father, enjoying retirement in Florida—remarried, someone said. Maybe he would never come back here. If he did, his mourners would have to bring a welder to open the tomb. "But if this is where the homeless person is staying, what were you welding before?"

"Before what? I just got here," Wally said. "I wasn't welding anything before."

Mysterious welders in the cemetery. Random shaving cream. It was worse than yuppies and their dogs, thought Mother Grey. She crammed the camping equipment into the rucksack and rolled and tied the sleeping bag. Later she would find the homeless person, doubtless one of her deranged alcoholic Vietnam veterans, and give him his stuff back. Poor man, it was probably all the property he had in the world. Right now she would go and catch up with the Smiths.

She found Mark wandering all alone and forlorn. "Even the weeds are different here," he said. "I haven't seen weeds like this since I was six years old. Did you ever think how many things happen without being recorded?"

"What sort of things?"

"I don't know. Events so small that nobody ever speaks of them. And when the last person dies who remembers what happened, it's as though it never happened at all. Have you seen Shannon, by the way?" he said.

"No. I thought she was with you."

6

The eastern border of the cemetery, the edge closest to the top of the hill, was fenced with chain link, and the access road was gated. Through this gate were the higher elevations of Fishersville, houses and streets, but not jammed up close together like the houses and streets down by the river. Here on the hill there was plenty of space for big wild yards, driveways, garages, even a small herd of white-tailed deer that wandered in the night and ate the garden plantings.

It was here by the chain-link gate that Shannon Smith came upon John Ferryman, gazing out across the cemetery at the town below. As she approached him, she thought him intensely picturesque. His weathered face, gilded by the westering sun, was like the face of a noble sea captain standing on the bridge of his ship facing the oncoming storm. But, no, the saying was "Red sky at night, sailor's delight," wasn't it? Okay, then, the sea captain was facing the prospect of excellent weather, but maybe a hard time when he got into port. Anyway, those could be storm clouds coming.

"Hello, Mr. Ferryman," she said, waking him out of his reverie.

"Oh, hello there," he said. "Mary Agnes's granddaughter."

"Shannon. It's beautiful, isn't it?" she said, following his gaze out over the valley.

"Sometimes I can't even stand to look," he said.

Sea captain, definitely. A sensitive sea captain. "Do you come out here often to look at the town?"

He chuckled. "Not what I'm doing out here. Had to check on something."

"The weather?"

"The latest from the teenagers. Somebody told me they turned some more tombstones over, and I wanted to go see while it was still light."

"You take care of the cemetery?"

"I like to keep an eye on it, me and a couple of other neighbors. Vandalism went way down after we started watching. You should have seen it before. The teenagers were raising hell."

"Did you find any damage this time?"

"No."

"I see one," she said. About ten feet from where she stood, an old granite grave marker had tipped off its pedestal and lay facedown in the grass.

"Not vandalism," he said. "That's frost heave." He swung the gate open—it wasn't locked—and went to the fallen gravestone. "The water gets into these cracks," he said, pointing to the place where the stone was faulted. "Then it freezes. Stone cracks off."

"Oh."

"Costs a lot of money to put them back up. Heavy equipment. The Friends of Mount Outlook do fund-raising drives every so often." He turned his eyes on her face, a searching sort of gaze. "Can you come over to my house and see me for a minute?"

She was thinking, *Should I go with this man? I hardly know him.* He could see that. "I just want to talk to somebody who knew Mary Agnes," he said.

"Actually, so do I," Shannon said.

He led her to his house, straight through the gate and across the road. Brick with a gabled roof, it was much like the houses back in town, except that it had an acre or so of lawns and shrubbery, a driveway, and a garage big enough for an old car and a pickup truck. As he sorted out his house key, she noticed his hands, the thick broken nails, the coarse skin with dirt and concrete ground in so deep that washing would never remove it, then his shoes, heavy yellow lace-up work boots with reinforced toes, lumps of yellow clay and light gray concrete clinging around the stitched seams of the blunt soles. He scraped off the mud onto the edge of his back doorstep, and then she noticed the doorstep itself. It was polished granite, almost like a gravestone.

"Come in," he said. "Can I get you some coffee or something?"

"A cup of tea would be good," she said, and followed him into the kitchen. A bit of framed needlepoint hung on the wall: "Penny's Kitchen." She wondered where Penny was.

"It's amazing how much you look like Mary Agnes," he said. "Same hair and everything."

"This style is back again," Shannon said, patting her curls. "I didn't do the pompadour, though. Nana wore hers in a pompadour."

"She was a lovely woman," he said, filling the teakettle. "And so are you. Hmh." This last grunt of annoyance seemed to be directed at the plumbing, which continued to make sounds after he turned the tap off. The low throbbing hum changed into a screeching sound, followed by a loud water hammer.

Shannon assumed the old man was embarrassed by the vagaries of his house's plumbing. "A good plumber can fix that for you," she said. "We used to have—"

"It's not that. Somebody's using my shower," he said. The slap of wet bare feet came down the hall. They both turned to stare at the doorway, and a man appeared, wearing only a grimy towel. He was in his late thirties, bearded, wiry, with crude dark blue tattoos and a deep tan that appeared only on his arms, neck, and head.

"Hi, Dad," he said. "Sorry to intrude. I didn't realize you were entertaining a lady friend."

"The hell are you doing here?"

"Don't worry. I only came to take one last shower. I'll just get my clothes and get out." He opened the door to the dryer and removed some things.

"Don't take nothin' else but the shower. I told you the last time, you weren't welcome here. I still haven't replaced the TV. But I guess you noticed. Probably you were looking for it."

"Dad, I'm a new man. I would never rip you off again."

"Just get dressed and get out. Don't come back."

The son began to dress himself, standing right there in the kitchen. First he pulled his shirt over his head. His voice was muffled through the fabric. "Don't worry about me, Dad." Shannon averted her face just before he dropped the towel. "I have friends now," he said. "We have big plans."

"That was you, wasn't it, camping out in the mausoleum?" the father said. "Scaring old ladies?"

"But, see, I don't have to do that anymore." He was fastening his shoes. It was okay for her to look at him again; he was wearing his pants. "Things have changed," he said. "I'm on a roll. Pretty soon I can send you what I owe you. I'll be in Vegas, anybody wants me."

"Nobody here wants you," the father said. "I'm through. You can call me if you ever get straight, Ronnie."

"Have a nice day yourself," Ronnie said, and slammed the back door.

"Sorry about that. Ronnie doesn't belong here, and he knows it. He ought to be in rehab someplace."

"I think I'd better go," Shannon said. "My own dad will be waiting for me."

"No tea?"

"Not this time."

"Maybe we can get together later."

"Maybe. I think we're going back to Phoenix tomorrow though."

"I'll see you out, anyway." When she stepped out John Ferryman's back door, the storm clouds had completely covered the setting sun and were now advancing into the clear sky over their heads, a ragged edge the color of slate. "It's going to rain," he said. "You'd better hurry."

He stood on the back step to watch her go down the access road. As she glanced back, John Ferryman absently wiped his feet again and spit on the step, almost like a ritual that he performed routinely without thinking about it anymore.

Shannon's father was sitting in the rental car with the engine running.

"Did you find the memorial stone?" she asked.

"No. I'm not sure it ever existed. Where have you been?"

"The old ladies said it existed. It sounded really pretty. It has a ship carved on it."

"It isn't there. Where were you?"

"I went to see John Ferryman."

The first big drops of rain began to fall on the windshield. "Who?"

"I met him in the Acme," she said. "I told you. Nana's old beau."

A streak of lightning ripped the slate-colored cloud mass away in the west. Shannon counted four seconds before the rumble and boom came. Rain lashed the car. Mark wasn't preparing to drive anywhere. He was just sitting and staring, figuring something out. "You said he was a concrete worker, right? The one who put the new floor in the Acme."

"John Ferryman. Yes."

"Of course. The key to the whole thing."

"What?"

"Don't go near him again."

"Why?"

"I can't tell you," Mark said. "A feeling I have. Something I almost remember."

"I think he's nice."

"Think what you want. Just don't go near him."

After breakfast the next day, Mother Grey went downtown, where everyone in Fishersville could be found on a Saturday morning, looking for the owner of the camping equipment. The homeless were in a sense her mission, and so she did not feel that they should be robbed of their possessions, no matter how untidy they might be in their personal habits. No one could tell her who the illicit camper might be until she ran into Nathan Hertz at the corner of Bridge and Main streets. In wilder days Nathan had lived among the homeless in the Hotel Ford, a collection of junked cars on the north side of Reeker's Hill. For six months now Nathan had been sober, but he still kept up with the Hotel Ford community.

"That's Ferryman's stuff," he told her, when she explained that the rucksack on her back belonged to the person who had been camping in the cemetery.

"John Ferryman?" She had trouble picturing the tough old contractor swaddling himself in nylon and down and going to sleep in a tomb.

"Ronnie. John's son," said Nathan. "John wouldn't let him in after he got out of jail the last time. You want me to give him this?"

"Will you be seeing him?"

"I might. If the door to his last crib was welded shut like you say, he'll probably show up on the hill." He put his hand on the rolled-up sleeping bag, feeling the nice soft down. "If I don't see him, I know plenty of people who would like to have it."

"Oh. Um—" Charity was always praiseworthy, but Mother Grey felt uncomfortable giving away other people's things without their permission.

"Hey, there goes old Ronnie now." She followed his pointing finger (grimy under the nail) to a slim, tousle-headed figure in jeans and a T-shirt nearly a block away, sauntering down Bridge Street in the direction of the river. "Yo!" he bellowed. "Yo! Ronnie!!" The figure did not stop, turn, or respond in any way. "I'll get him for you, Mother Vinnie," Nathan said, and as she watched, he went tearing across the street in pursuit.

Before Nathan could reach him, a sleek black car pulled up to the curb next to Ron Ferryman (if that was who it was). The passenger-side door opened as though of itself; the slim man got in; and the black car went zipping over the narrow bridge to Pennsylvania at twice the legal limit of fifteen miles an hour.

Nathan was panting when she caught up with him. "Nice car. Ronnie's got himself a rich friend."

Mother Grey knew very little about cars. "What was it?"

"Brand-new Mercedes-Benz SL-500. Seventy-five-thousand-dollar car."

Certainly a lot of money to spend on transportation. But the driver's face was of greater concern to Mother Grey. A fleeting glimpse was all she caught of that profile, and yet she was almost certain it was Mark Smith.

Shannon came into the hotel room and found her father sorting out his clothes on the bed. "What are you doing?"

"Packing. We're getting out of here."

"But what about Nana's ashes?"

"Honey, it's not important. She's gone. She won't ever know or care what we did with her ashes."

"I'll know. Besides, I'm not leaving here without finding out what happened to Grandfather."

Mark mumbled something Shannon couldn't hear.

"Don't you care?" she said.

"No, I don't care." His tone was flat.

"You know already, don't you?"

"What?"

"You know, and you aren't telling me."

"Why would I do that?"

"I don't know. But I can see that you know something you aren't telling me. What's this business about Mr. Ferryman?"

He froze. Only his eyes moved, from the door to the shaving kit in his hands and back again. *My father has shifty eyes.* Shannon had never noticed it before. Then he sighed and said, "Sugar, it's time to go home now. Go on back to your room and pack your things. The plane leaves for Phoenix in three hours."

"But I just came from seeing Claudine."

"Yes?"

"Her friend got a reading on Grandfather."

"Claudine's friend got a reading." Mark resumed his packing. It was a ritual with him, to fold each garment just so, to put each into the carry-on bag in its appointed order and place. It was almost as though he believed that if he did it right every time, not only would his clothes not wrinkle, but the gods of travel would be in some way propitiated and grant him a safe journey.

They couldn't just leave like this. "Daddy, Claudine's

friend is a psychic. He said we would find Grandfather in a high place surrounded by light, with an angel at his right hand."

Mark frowned and shook his head. "That's easy enough," he said. "He's dead. But it's not to the purpose, since what we wanted to find was his mortal remains, sometime in this life and preferably before tomorrow. I have business back in Phoenix, sweetheart. Please pack now."

"So you won't tell me what happened to my grandfather."

"I don't know, sweetheart. I was six years old."

"I think you do know. I think somewhere in your mind you remember."

He zipped up the bag. "No, actually, I don't." He put his head in the bathroom and checked under the used towels one last time. "Please go pack your things," he said. "Don't forget the shampoo and soap. They can't use it again. You might as well have it."

"Okay, but I want you to see Claudine's friend before we go," she said.

"Why? He already told us his, uh, reading."

"He's a licensed hypnotist, Dad. He helps people recover lost memories."

"Oh, for—"

"See him for five minutes. We have plenty of time before our plane leaves. The airport is only an hour away. I'll go and pack while you check out, and then we'll drop by and see this man at the New Age Center."

"For five minutes."

"He can help you remember."

But she could see it in his face; he didn't want to

remember. "It won't even take me five minutes to tell him what I have to say."

The New Age Center was a tall brick building, only three stories high but seeming higher because of the scale of the rooms inside and the height of the ceilings. It had been built in the nineteenth century as some sort of temple of commerce. Nowadays there was an arty import shop on the ground floor facing the street and to one side of that a door covered with tacked-up leaflets, cards, and handwritten notices of New Age activities taking place inside.

The ceilings were so high that the climb up the stairs to the second floor seemed endless. The steps were wooden, original with the building, scooped out in the middle by the tread of many feet. The balustrade was bigger around than normal, and higher, not to be gripped by ordinary human hands. Giants of industry must have used these stairs when they were first built.

But Mark's feet were dragging. Shannon noticed that he was going more slowly up those strange overscale stairs than he had up the narrow steps to his parents' old bedroom—the Bad Room in the House of Evil, as she had come to think of it.

"Hypnosis is like lancing a boil," Claudine whispered to Shannon when they arrived. "All the ugly stuff comes oozing out and nothing is left inside but good health. Don't worry about him. Barton will fix everything."

After that disgusting, gross comparison of her father's psyche to an infected pimple, Shannon began to have very serious doubts indeed about Claudine's judgment in these matters, but before she had a chance to express them, the massive door in front of them swung open and the great man emerged.

He was not wearing a long black robe with stars and moons on it, except maybe in his mind, but rather a tweed coat over a knitted polo shirt and khakis. As Shannon put out her hand, he took it in his own, applying firm but gentle pressure, putting his other hand on top. His hands were warm and tingly, very spiritual. He had bug eyebrows; they stuck straight out from his forehead and curved over his eyes.

"Come with me," the great man said to Mark. "You girls will have to wait outside."

"For five minutes," said Mark. "Don't go anywhere, Shannon. We have a plane to catch."

". . . and when you wake up you will feel calm, relaxed, and happy. You will remember everything that happened, everything you told me while you were under hypnosis. Wake up now, Mark."

And so Mark woke up and remembered everything. Chiefly he remembered regressing to the age of six and reliving the last time he ever saw his father, covered with blood and screaming. Yet he was unable to make any sense out of it.

Before that, he had gone back to the night when a man visited his mother. This was an unusual occurrence. While it was true that his father was hardly ever home, his mother did not customarily entertain other men.

But this man—

This man smoked a pipe. Mark smelled it.

This man cried. Mark could hear him snuffling, hear his voice breaking.

This man told his mother right out that he had never loved his wife. He said he had only married her because . . . because . . . well, why do any of us marry?

"Was the man still there in the morning?"

Mark could remember seeing no sign of him. He never saw him again either, at least not to recognize him. Recognize his voice, that is. He never did *see* him.

"Did the man have a name?"

'I didn't hear her call him anything. I went back to sleep myself after a while. You know how it is when grown-ups are making noise in the middle of the night. You try to sleep." But he knew. It was John Ferryman, who loved Mark's mother.

"Tell me, Mark, was this the same night as the flood?"

"No. No, long before."

The hypnotist was very soothing. "All right now, I want you to bring yourself into the night of the flood. Just before the flood came. What are you doing now?"

"Sleeping. I'm sleeping in my bed."

"Start with the noises."

"My mother and father are shouting."

"What are they saying?"

"I can't hear."

"They shout a lot?"

"No, they never shout." That was why it was so scary. They never shouted. Most of the time Dad wasn't even home.

"And do you get out of bed because of the shouting?"

"Yes." The dark room, the little fuzzy rug, finding his slippers by the toy box. Out into the hallway.

Up the stairs, slowly. Light coming through a crack in the door.

A crash, a scream. His father screaming! The door

crack widens, a knife of light. Framed in the door, his mother. Blood on her shoe. Behind her his dad with red all over his arm and down the front of his white shirt.

Back to bed. Get under the covers. Be safe there.

Markie, get up. Your father is dead.

7

It was half an hour to the minute between the time Shannon's father disappeared behind the big oak door and the time he came out again. Claudine went away after ten minutes—to go shopping, she said—and left Shannon alone in the chilly dark hallway.

When he came out, he was not the same man.

"How do you feel, Daddy?"

He blinked. "I am afloat on a sea of . . . I dunno what the hell I'm afloat on," he said. "Maybe I'm not even afloat."

"Did you remember what happened to Grandfather?"

"He was murdered."

"Oh, no." *He's gone completely crazy,* she thought.

"Your friend John Ferryman killed him the night of the flood and buried his body under the Acme."

Maybe if I get him home right away, he'll be okay again. "Let's go, Dad," she said. "The car is right across the street. We can—"

"Didn't you hear what I said? That old man killed my father. I can't let my father go unavenged."

This friend of Claudine's has driven him mad. Why did I make him come here?

"We've got to go and see the police."

What shall I do?

They descended the endless staircase and went out into the sunny street. *Maybe if I get Mother Grey.* "Let's go back and see Mother Grey," Shannon said. "She can tell us where the police station is."

"Anybody can tell us where the police station is," Mark said. "He can tell us where it is." He was speaking of old Horace Burkhardt, coming down the street toward them as fast as he could. Before they had a chance to stop him and ask the whereabouts of the police station, there came a terrific crash, and from away behind the bank a cloud of dust or smoke rose up. "What was that?"

"The Acme," said Horace Burkhardt, nor did he slacken his pace. "Come on!" he called over his shoulder. "You gotta see this! They're pulling it down."

"The Acme! That's great! Maybe they'll uncover my father's bones!"

"Daddy—"

"No, this is wonderful. Justice at last. There's no statute of limitations on murder, is there? Let's go."

"Daddy, I don't think you should go on like this."

"Why not?"

Because it's crazy, Daddy. This is a crazy idea. People will notice that you've lost your mind, and then maybe they'll lock you up. She fumbled for something he might accept. "People might think—how will they know who put the body there? People might say—"

"What?"

That you're mad. But, no, that wouldn't persuade him to stop this. "They might think that Mary Agnes, you know, killed him or something."

He stared as though it was she who was losing her mind. "Why would anybody imagine that my mother killed my father?"

"Husbands and wives kill each other all the time."

He patted her shoulder. "They won't think that. I'll tell them the truth. Find a policeman, sweetheart. I'll meet you at the Acme."

Mother Grey was raking the cigarette packs and soda cups out of the bushes in front of St. Bede's when Shannon came running up to her. "You've got to help me. My dad sent me to find a police officer."

"Whatever for?"

"There's no time to explain."

"Of course there is," Mother Grey insisted. "There's always time to explain." Miscommunication was at the root of most of the ills of the world. The silly notion of having no time to explain was something thought up by lazy movie directors to enable them to cut directly to the chase. Speaking of the chase, there it was, parked a block and a half away, waiting to catch speeders: Jack Kreevitch's patrol car. With luck he would be in it, although at times the short-handed local police propped a dummy, donated by a local men's store, in the driver's seat. "Come on. You can tell me about it as we go."

They walked briskly. As Shannon unfolded the tale of

her father's mad obsession, Mother Grey saw that it was indeed Jack Kreevitch sitting behind the wheel of the police cruiser. Traffic slowed at the sight of him, which was good, since the tee-ball league was having a game at the ballfield a few blocks farther on.

Mother Grey knocked on the passenger window. "We need you, Jack!" Shannon was blushing. Could it be that she felt silly? *The sky is falling, cried Chicken Little!*

He reached over and rolled the window down. "What can I do for you, Mother Vinnie?"

"Would you come with us? They're digging up the floor of the Acme." She glanced at Shannon. "It might be a professional call for you."

"How do you mean?"

"My friend here has an idea that her grandfather might have been buried under the slab forty years ago."

"No kidding."

"Actually, no, I don't believe that," Shannon said. "But my father seems to believe it, and he sent me to find you."

"Who is your father?"

"Mark Smith. Jim Smith's son."

Kreevitch frowned in thought. "Would that be Jimmy Smith the accountant, or Jim Smith who teaches at the high school?"

"You don't remember this Jim Smith, Jack. He died before you were born," Mother Grey said.

"And they put his body under the Acme?" He scratched his head, pushing his hat back. "I know this town used to be kind of wild, but bodies under the Acme is a new one on me."

Shannon was jigging nervously. "We need to hurry. I

promised my dad. Just in case they turn up some bones, he wants you to be there."

"At the Acme?"

"I promised we would meet him. Actually I think he might be sick. I don't want to leave him alone."

"I know you're busy, Jack, but can you spare us a few minutes?" Mother Grey said.

"Sure," Jack Kreevitch said. "If they turn up a body, I wouldn't want to miss it." He dragged his fellow officer, the dummy, out of the backseat, propped it up in the driver's seat, and put his hat on top. "Officer Mathews will watch this road while I'm gone."

People were gathering at the Acme, mothers with their babies in strollers, tourists, oldsters with canes, honeymooners holding hands. Large-scale destruction always seems to draw a crowd. Jack Kreevitch circled around behind the parking lot to get a better look at the excavation.

Shannon and Mother Grey looked for Mark. "Tell me something," Mother Grey said. "Does your father ever drive a black Mercedes-Benz SL-500?"

Shannon gave a mirthless laugh. "I wish."

"Strange," said Mother Grey. She greeted Mabel Weeds and her cronies from Delio's, craning their necks on the fringes of the gathering. She knew all their names now. They returned her greeting.

Mabel took her by the hand and with the other hand gripped Shannon's arm. "Don't forget," she whispered. "I have something for you."

Oh, rats, they had forgotten. "We'll come over this afternoon," Mother Grey said. "I promise." Still they didn't see Mark. Peter Susswald appeared in the crowd at her elbow, and Mother Grey remembered the cemetery work party she had promised to join, and that it was to be today. Rats again. "When are we meeting on Mount Outlook?" she said to him.

"One o'clock, but they'll wait. It isn't every day they tear down the Acme. I love a good demolition, don't you?"

"Well, no," Mother Grey replied. "Not exactly."

"You didn't come here for fun?"

"No. We're, ah, here to see what turns up." She patted Shannon on the shoulder. The girl was gazing distractedly at the crowd. Still no Mark.

"Expecting anything in particular?" Susswald said.

"Bones," Shannon said. Her wild look was almost comical.

"Bones? Here? Whose bones?"

"Somebody thinks Shannon's grandfather was buried under the concrete slab," Mother Grey explained. *You see, there is always time to explain.* A shadow passed over them, perhaps a cloud moving over the face of the sun, perhaps a large airplane. With a sound like the growl of a large menacing animal, the bulldozer operator started his engine and gunned it.

"And who might her grandfather be?" Susswald had always been fascinated by local genealogy.

"James Smith," Shannon said.

"Not the accountant or the teacher, nor yet the electrician," Mother Grey hastened to add.

Susswald waggled his bushy eyebrows meaningfully. "Wouldn't be James Waring Smith, would it?"

"Why, yes," Shannon said. "How did you know?"

" 'Nineteen twenty-three to 1955, beloved husband of Mary Agnes Smith,' " Susswald said.

"That's him, all right," said Mother Grey.

"There's a gravestone on Mount Outlook. He's buried there," Susswald said.

"No, he's not. They say he was lost in the flood, and his body was never found," Shannon said.

"The stone is more of a memorial," Mother Grey said.

"And it isn't up there, either," Shannon said. "We looked all over the cemetery."

"It must be there. It's on my list," Susswald said. He drew a rolled comb-bound booklet from his jacket pocket and opened it to the third page or so. "See here. 'Stone of polished brown granite, thirty by twenty by seven inches, across the top a frieze of a ship in full sail.' It's on the Rabson plot, about twelve feet north by northeast of the marble angel." He had to shout, because the sounds of the demolition were growing louder.

"What list is this?" Mother Grey asked. It had been typed and then bound with one of those patent binders that people use for fancy presentations.

"I made a copy of some records Mrs. van Buskirk had."

"Have you seen the memorial with the ship?" Shannon asked.

"Not yet, but I will. We're going to photograph all the important ornaments and statuary today. That's what today's work party is for."

"May I come too?" Shannon said.

"Please do. Everyone's welcome. We need all the help we can get."

"This will make a very interesting art project," Mother Grey said. Susswald was a prominent player in the artistic life of the town, the poetry society, the painters' guild.

"Gorgeous," Susswald agreed. "But that's not the primary purpose. I'm afraid it has to be done as a theft deterrent. I don't know whether you've heard, but a number of graveyards have been robbed in recent months. Mount Outlook may need protection."

"My word."

"Old Mr. Ferryman keeps an eye on the east gate and watches the cemetery as best he can—he's one of our group—but he can't always be there, or see everything that goes on."

Jack Kreevitch appeared. He had been strolling around the crowd of onlookers, noticing everything, as was his professional habit, and now that the talk in Mother Grey's little group was turning to crime, he was back in their midst. "Cemetery thefts," he said. "I guess that'll be the next thing."

"You heard about it, right, Jack? Definitely the work of professionals," Susswald said. "Bringing in heavy equipment to carry away statuary. Taking advantage of lax security. I'm sure you've seen the stories."

Kreevitch bristled. "I don't know what you call lax. Every Saturday we post a man in the cemetery all night, ever since that rash of vandalism we had."

"Saturday night, yes, but not at other times. I don't mean to criticize the police, Jack—you have the whole town to watch, and live people come first, of course. It's just that we may have a problem before long."

"Could be. We'll keep our eyes open." Kreevitch shifted his gaze, looking for a way to change the subject. "So, Mother Vinnie," he said at last. "Whaddeya hear from Dave?"

"Nothing much," she said.

"You two aren't, er—"

"No, we aren't, er." How was it that whenever Jack

Kreevitch saw her, he persisted in asking about Dave? He knew perfectly well that she had a complete and satisfying life apart from Dave. Her time with Dave, sweet though it might have been, was a passing interlude. Passing and now in fact past. Dave had no part anymore in her day-to-day existence. Dave was forgotten.

Completely.

Kreevitch rubbed the back of his neck. Was he embarrassed, or had a mosquito bitten him? "I guess you heard about Felicia."

Dave's ex-wife. "No. What?" But it was too noisy for conversation. *Putty putty putty nyaaah* went the bulldozer, backing up, rolling forward, smashing into the wall of the Acme. Cascading cinderblocks tumbled into the parking lot.

A baby began to scream, and its mother wheeled it away from the violence of the demolition, pushing its stroller between Mother Grey and Kreevitch. How it bellowed.

Mother Grey thought about Felicia. She had not seen Dave Dogg's ex-wife in years, not since the period after their divorce and before their on-again, off-again reconciliation. Mother Grey's best friend Deedee used to call Felicia Dave's yo-yo wife—the more he threw her out, the faster she came rolling back—but this was not entirely fair to Dave. Initially it was Felicia who had dumped him, taken Ricky, moved to West Windsor, and filed for divorce, saying she no longer wanted to be an inner-city policeman's wife. The murder rate in Trenton was rising in those days. Stressful for a homicide detective, as Dave himself acknowledged; he said he was difficult to live with, whatever that meant in practical terms. So Felicia dumped him. It was only a long time afterward, after her mother died, in fact, that she started drinking heavily and doing her yo-yo thing, bouncing in and out of Dave's life.

Indeed, the last time Mother Grey actually laid eyes on her, she was merely Dave's ex-wife, the mother of his son, a woman from his past, not drinking yet, or between binges. She must have been sober, or Dave never would have let Ricky get in the car with her. A summer evening—how well Mother Grey remembered it. She and Dave and young Ricky were lounging on the steps at Dave's place, pleasantly tired from a day at the shore—Dave's hand warm in her hand, the smell of suntan lotion, sand between her toes, sunburn tightening the skin across her cheekbones. Felicia pulled up across the street and honked the horn. Mother Grey reached out and touched the boy's hair, damp and salty. Felicia tooted again, and Ricky crossed over and got in the car; Mother Grey had watched him go with a curious sense of loss, which she could still feel when she let herself.

So. Was something amiss with Felicia now? What could Jack Kreevitch have meant by that look he gave her?

She drew breath to ask him, but it was still too noisy in the Acme parking lot to talk. A knot of gapers forced their way into the space between them, shrieking and pointing to the newly exposed high-water mark on the far wall of what was left of the Acme. Then with a great clanking and crashing, the power shovel hooked its claw under the raw edge of the concrete floor and lifted. The floor fell away in scabby chunks.

Suddenly, in the black earth underneath, a long bone appeared that could have been a human femur.

Dead silence fell over the crowd. The power shovel stopped its digging.

"Bingo," Jack Kreevitch muttered.

And there was Mark Smith, ten feet from where they stood, staring into the pit of dirt like a man who doubts his own senses.

"Daddy," said Shannon. She went to him and took his arm.

"Then it's true," he said.

"You didn't think it was true?" she said. Mother Grey helped her pull him back away from the hole.

He turned and saw Jack Kreevitch standing there in uniform, staring at him, and began talking to him almost as though he thought he'd been talking to him before and meant to continue the conversation. "Yes, I know I was the one who insisted that my father was under the slab," he said. "But, you know, up to now, I don't think I really believed it."

"Yet you sent your daughter to bring me here," said Kreevitch.

"Yes," he said. "But that was just in case."

Ambivalence. This was something that Mother Grey understood. Clearly what Mark really wanted was to discover that nothing out of the way had happened on the day of his father's death; that on the contrary he had lain down to sleep the long sleep as a result of perfectly natural and unremarkable causes, or had died a hero defending his own family or rescuing another, and had passed out of the land of the living with a blessing on his lips for Mary Agnes and for his son. So naturally Mark insisted that his father had been violently done to death. This insistence would surely provoke a denial from someone who knew the truth, a denial he would eventually come to believe.

But here were these bones.

And here was the police officer he had sent Shannon to find. "My father was murdered," Mark said to him. "See there? His remains are down in that hole."

Kreevitch produced a notebook and began to write down a report. Bones made the whole thing official. "May I have your full name, sir?"

Mark identified himself and repeated his charges, adding details.

"I wouldn't jump to any conclusions just yet, Mr. Smith," Kreevitch said. "We turned up some remains, is all. We don't even know they're human remains, much less your father's." He folded the notebook into a pocket and plied his radio, calling for backup and the homicide investigation team.

"I know those are my father's bones," Mark said. "You know it too, don't you?"

"Keep calm," Kreevitch said. "One thing at a time." He took out some yellow tape and draped it around the hole, shooing away the bystanders.

The workmen were grumbling. "Just take a break, okay?" the officer said to them. "As soon as someone from the homicide team takes a look at the site, you can start digging again, okay? And maybe someone from Trenton too." The workmen disposed themselves grudgingly in attitudes of loitering; the shovel operator climbed down out of his cab and lit up a cigarette.

Parked at the curb was John Ferryman's red pickup truck. The old man sat behind the wheel, himself enjoying a cigarette, with the windows rolled up to keep out the dust of demolition.

"There he is," Mark said.

Kreevitch followed Mark's pointing finger. "Who would that be, sir?"

"The man who killed my father and buried his body under the Acme."

"John Ferryman?"

"Right."

"The oldsters say he put that cement floor in," Mother Grey piped up. "For what it's worth." Kreevitch made a knot in the last bit of police tape and went slowly over to the truck, followed closely by Mark Smith, Shannon, and finally Mother Grey, torn between curiosity and reluctance to intrude.

Kreevitch tapped on the window and cast a meaningful look inside. The old man rolled it down.

"Can I talk to you for a minute, Mr. Ferryman?"

"Sure, son. What about?"

"They tell me you buried something under the Acme."

"What? When?"

"In 1955."

John Ferryman frowned and appeared to look inward, rooting around in his mind for something that happened forty years before. "You mean the spoiled meat?" he said at last.

"Was it spoiled meat?"

"There were a couple lamb carcasses that were in the flood. They didn't make the garbage collection so the manager told me just put 'em in the ground and cover them up when I laid the new floor."

"I see."

"You're gonna arrest me for that, you'll have to arrest

Sam Banniger too, Jack. He's the one told me to do it. Of course he's dead, oh, it must be fifteen years now."

"Uh-huh."

"Isn't there some kind of statute of limitations on littering?"

"I wouldn't be bothering you if it was just littering, Mr. Ferryman."

"What, you think I killed one of them lambs?"

His cool self-possession was too much for Mark Smith. "You killed my father, you son of a bitch!"

John Ferryman looked Mark Smith up and down; his pale eyes narrowed with contempt. He turned back to Jack Kreevitch. "I can't do nothing here till they finish this digging. Are you going to hold it up on account of a couple of lamb carcasses?"

"'Fraid so, Mr. Ferryman."

"Then I guess I'll go home," he said. "You want me for anything, you know where I live." He rolled up the window again and started the engine. Mark gaped with disbelief at the back of the muddy truck, disappearing up the hill.

"He's getting away!"

"Let go of my uniform, Mr. Smith. He isn't going anywhere."

"He's getting away! He's running!"

"I don't think so. His house is here, his business is here. And until we get confirmation from the lab that those bones are human, I haven't anything to charge him with."

"Charge him with murder! The dirty bastard killed my father and buried his body under the concrete! I had to grow up fatherless because of what he did!"

"Now, now, Mr. Smith."

"Aren't you going to do anything?"

"One thing at a time."

"You're all in this together, I see."

"What do you mean?"

"One hand washes the other. Everybody here is related to everybody else anyway, I can see that. Sure, you don't want to arrest your own uncle."

"Calm down, Mr. Smith. Nobody's my uncle. We do things according to procedure. First we need to see what these bones are, and if it turns out they're even human bones, then we need to make a positive identification, and after that if there's really a problem, we'll look for the person responsible."

"I told you who's responsible."

"Don't worry. Justice will prevail. It usually does."

"I know how to see for myself that justice prevails, if you people won't do it."

"Try to relax, sir. Above all, don't make threats."

"The death of my father will not go unavenged."

"Let's go, Daddy," said Shannon, pulling him by the arm again.

He noticed the concern on her face and understood that she thought he was raving, which made him madder than ever. "The son of a bitch murdered my father," he insisted. "He's getting away."

8

Some stayed and jostled for good places to gape at the hole under the Acme, and some went abroad to spread strange tales of long-buried bodies. Mother Grey headed for the rectory to walk the dog. As she hoofed along, unusual traffic went speeding toward the Acme: dark vehicles from the county prosecutor's office, a white van with a television dish on top. Fishersville would be in the evening news.

Headed in the opposite direction, the Friends of Mount Outlook were going up the hill in hiking shoes and duck boots, cameras slung over their shoulders, to slog through the mud for the spring field day. *I'll meet them up there,* Mother Grey thought, *when I finish these chores.* It would be her first Mount Outlook field day. In previous seasons she had resisted Peter Susswald's blandishments, being too busy, but today her life had reached—could it be possible?—a lull.

As she understood it, their purpose today was to do cleanup and recording work, spiffing and photographing the more important ornaments of Mount Outlook. Peter touted it as a sort of picnic. He had invited everyone over for wine and cheese afterward in his tiny restored jewel-box house across the street from the cemetery's broad front steps.

She let herself into the rectory and dropped the camping equipment by the front door. Towser made a big fuss over her, as always. The light on the answering machine was blinking, and when she pushed the play button, the voice of Dave Dogg said, "It's me, Vinnie. Could you call me?"

Again. Whatever could he want, after three months of silence? Three months, two days, and fourteen hours, to be precise. If she closed her eyes, she could still see the back of him going out her kitchen door, the afternoon sun glinting off his baseball hat, his shoulders, as always, expressive, this time of disappointment mixed with firm resolve.

It might have been their last fight. She could almost bring herself to hope it was. What had started out as a sweet romantic relationship had become something very painful to her.

"It's not that I'm jerking you around," he insisted.

"Dave, you've been jerking me around for years."

"Ah, Vinnie."

"I'm not going to sink into one of these relationships of romantic suffering with you, Dave. I don't enjoy erotic angst. I hate it. I have better things to do with my time."

"You may have better things to do with your time,

Vinnie, but you don't hate it. You love it. What you hate is loving it."

She took a deep breath. Was this what men were all about? No. "Stephen Grey was a decent man. He treated me decently."

He recoiled as though she had slapped him. "I'm sorry. I'm sorry I'm not Stephen. I'm sorry he's dead."

Never before had she thrown her deceased husband in Dave's face. Of course Stephen was a better man. He hadn't lived long enough to mess up. "Dave, I didn't mean to say that. I know you aren't Stephen. You aren't supposed to be Stephen."

"You probably aren't going to understand or believe this, Vinnie, but the reason I can't leave Felicia has a lot to do with you, with your moral standards. Felicia is— what do you call it in your sermons?—broken, a broken person. How can I dump her? What would happen to her?"

"I don't know, Dave, but you're going to have to choose one of us and let the other one go. Flip a coin. Try stone-paper-scissors, best two out of three."

"Do you think anybody would live with an alcoholic for fun?" he said. "A person would have to be a lot sicker than I am."

"Nobody said you were sick."

"I am. I'm sick."

"Maybe we're all sick," she said. "Do you realize that what you're doing is inviting me to compete for you by collapsing in some way, so that I'll be in worse shape than Felicia and you can leave her with a good con- science?"

"No, I'm not. I would never do that. I'm not like that."

"That's how it feels. I can feel a pull: 'Cut your wrists,

have some sort of breakdown, then you can have Dave.' This isn't what I want out of a relationship. I need to be nourished and supported. I need someone who will encourage me to be better."

"I'm not trying to tear you down. I'm trying to do the right thing."

"Go home, Dave."

"You don't know what it is, do you?"

"What?"

"Life with a drunk."

"Then leave her. I don't want to hear your complaints."

"Okay. Right. Forget I said anything." He put on his hat. "See you around."

Three months, two days, fourteen hours, and twenty minutes. She dialed his number. Again no one answered. She stuffed her gardening gloves and camera into her handbag and started up the hill to meet Peter Susswald and the Friends of Mount Outlook.

The Fishersville bookseller was sitting at the center of a circle of cemetery devotees on the white steps of the cemetery, his camera slung around his neck, his notebook in his hand, his face turned toward his own house across the street and the river valley beyond it. His acolytes were a mixed bag: a few middle-aged women older than Mother Grey, two artistic-looking men, and a couple of Mother Grey's parishioners: Martine Wellworth with her little boy Henry, and the ancient but game Delight van Buskirk, accompanied by her granddaughter Claudine. Martine grinned at her when she saw Mother Grey coming up the street, almost self-consciously, as though to say, "You've caught me again, out meeting people."

The Dusky Beauty, Dave always called her. She was certainly a beauty, and also African-American; Mother Grey was never able to decide whether calling Martine the Dusky Beauty was racially offensive. Probably, since he never did it to her face. Or maybe it was offensively sexist.

Several times of late Mother Grey had noticed Martine taking time off from her busy law practice to involve herself in the life of the town. Mother Grey suspected she was preparing to run for public office. It was one of those things she meant to gossip about with Dave. But then, Dave wasn't around these days.

"I guess this is about it," Peter said. "Everyone else must be watching them look for bodies under the Acme." He looked almost disappointed with the size of his group; normally there must have been more of them.

"Isn't John Ferryman going to be with us today?" one of the women said.

"He said he was, but something must have come up," Peter said. He counted the crowd again and began shuffling the papers in his hand, one pile for each Friend. "We should get a chance to see some really great things today," he said. "I haven't seen some of them myself yet. No fewer than five antique benches and three angel statues, plus a number of interesting headstones. You all have cameras, right?"

They said they did.

"Because if not, I have a couple of disposables here you can use." He gave out assignments. "I saved the section with the Wagonner mausoleum for you," he said to Mother Grey. "You had some kind of personal interest in it, didn't you?"

"In a measure," Mother Grey said. Her poor friend

Phyllis was buried there, the one who went mad. She had held her in her arms when she died. She looked up to see Shannon Smith coming to join their group, stretching her long legs in a power walk. Her father was not with her. Speaking of crazy people.

"What exactly do we need to photograph?" Mother Grey said. "Everything? Or simply everything of interest?"

"Everything on this list," Peter said. He gave her what appeared to be a photocopy of a page in his notebook, copied from Mrs. van Buskirk's list of notable features. "I guess you can—Hello, Shannon—I guess the two of you can take that section there, starting with that big copper beech tree and going all the way back to the fence. The Rabson plot is up there, so you should be able to locate your grandfather's memorial."

"Great," said Shannon. "I can take Dad up there and show it to him when he gets up. I talked him into lying down for a while at the hotel."

Peter stood up and ascended the steps; the others went before him, fanning out into the cemetery.

To each person there, the Mount Outlook Cemetery meant something different. To the preservationists—a hard-core group in Fishersville, where the itch to preserve was very strong—the old cemetery was a place dedicated to the grace and beauty of times past, times when it was widely believed that human beings could be creatures of dignity and nobility, even in death. They were there not only to clean and photograph the monuments but also to honor the men and women who lay under them. That these people were strangers to them, and long dead, was unimportant.

To young Henry Wellworth, the cemetery was the

place of his nightmares. As soon as he got far enough up the hill to see the headstones, he remembered. "I want to go home."

"What's wrong?" his mother said.

"I don't like it here. This is where the people live under the signs."

"What signs?" his mother asked.

"Those." He pointed to a row of grave markers.

"No one lives under those signs, Henry."

"Yes, they do, they live in the dirt, and if you walk on them, they stick their hand up and grab you by the leg." Embarrassed to death, Martine gave her sheet of assignments back to Peter, saying she would return later if she could get her husband to take care of Henry. *Unsupervised television-viewing*, thought Mother Grey, watching Martine buckle Henry into his car seat. People who live under the signs, indeed. She needed to have a talk with the Wellworths about monitoring that boy's entertainment.

To Delight van Buskirk, Mount Outlook was almost like home; here was the place where her husband slept, her parents, her sister, and two of her children. Being almost like home, keeping it tidy was important to her.

To her fey granddaughter, however, Mount Outlook was a haunt of evil spirits.

"But why ever would you think that these spirits are evil?" Delight argued. "They weren't evil when they were alive. They were just our neighbors."

"I feel it," the girl said. "Bad influences are here." She tied a long ribbon around her grandmother's neck, with two crystals and a bunch of dried herbs dangling from it. Then she began to hum and mumble.

"Now what are you doing?" Mrs. van Buskirk asked.

"It's a chant of protection," Claudine said.

"Silly child." The old lady tottered away to her sector, a patch low down on the hill specially selected by Peter so as not to tax her heart.

Shannon looked at Mother Grey's list of cemetery marvels and then at Mrs. van Buskirk, who was making her way down to the semicircular marble bench set into the hill in memory of the city merchant. Then she turned her eyes toward her own family plot. "I wish we had seen this list yesterday," she said. "Here's my grandfather's memorial, clearly described. Didn't Peter get this list from Mrs. van Buskirk?"

"She probably forgot she had it," Mother Grey said. "Old people forget things."

Down in the town the digging and smashing sounds began again, answered by the sound of a grinding engine over the brow of the hill. *This is the noisiest town*, she thought, and then, *They're digging again. Maybe they've satisfied themselves somehow that they aren't dealing with a crime scene.* That would be good. It was a point of pride in Fishersville that sixty years had passed between the last murder and the one before. It would have been a shame to spoil the record.

About the time that Mrs. van Buskirk began attacking the weeds around the great bench, another of the women was back at the steps again, pulling on Peter's sleeve. "It says here, 'a marble figure of two children, just beyond the iron fence on the other side of the beech tree,' " she said.

"That's right," he said.

"There's no iron fence there," she said. "Nor any marble children." The others began returning as well, all reporting things missing. Again they heard the faraway grinding of an engine, and a *zoop-bang* sound, perhaps of a truck door closing.

"I don't understand," Peter said. He looked at his notebook and back up the hill. *He understands, all right,* thought Mother Grey; *he just doesn't want to understand.* The cemetery had been robbed, the treasures taken before they could be photographed.

Last to come straggling back was Delight van Buskirk herself, official keeper of the list, her anti–evil spirit charms bouncing and bobbing.

"I did copy the right list, didn't I, Mrs. van Buskirk?" Peter said, still in denial. "Could I have made some mistake?"

"No mistake," she said, shaking her head.

The woman who sought the marble children spoke up. "Then where—"

"Gone," Mrs. van Buskirk said. "All gone. Everything that could be taken away. The grave robbers have been here before us."

Mother Grey and Shannon went up the hill to see how hard the Rabsons had been hit. In the face of the Wagonner mausoleum, a black empty hole gaped where the bronze door had been, the door that Wally Pascoe had welded shut the day before. Inside that violated space, evidence of further outrage: the stained glass lilies were missing, the frame broken out and the glass gone. Mother Grey came out into the light again and gazed as far as she could see at the rest of the cemetery. No iron railings were left at all, no benches, and no statues. The bronze doors had been removed from every tomb. On the Rabson plot nothing remained of the beautiful angel but a white marble hand, trodden into the mud.

Shannon picked it up, wiped it off, and handed it to

Mother Grey. This was what came of people with money thinking how nice it would be to have an angel in the garden. Never mind where it came from. Never mind that we're robbing the dead, despoiling irreplaceable treasures that belong, in a sense, to all the people. Mother Grey thought of the boys she had discovered once, prying lead weights off the sides of automobile wheels. When she asked them sternly what they were up to, they replied without the least consciousness of wrongdoing that they were getting sinkers for fishing. "They grow on car wheels," the biggest boy explained. So it was with graveyard ornaments; they grow in marble orchards.

Mother Grey's bitter meditation was broken by Claudine, who drifted wraithlike from behind the Wagonner mausoleum, babbling: "It's happening! Oh, no! It's happening!"

"What is?" Mother Grey said, not really expecting an answer; Claudine was having one of her fits.

It was Shannon who shouted and pointed: "Mother Vinnie! Look out!" She turned to see a beach ball rolling toward her, shiny and white, only it wasn't a beach ball; it was one of those polished stone spheres they put on memorial columns in cemeteries, solid rock, enormous, coming straight for her, faster and faster.

9

"Lamb bones."

Chief Harry, never one to miss an opportunity for fun, was busting the chops of Jack Kreevitch with the latest news from the county homicide people. Kreevitch had come back to the station to write his report on the excavation at the Acme, only to find that the homicide crew he left at the scene had reached their conclusion two minutes after their arrival and telephoned the chief.

"Lamb bones?"

"Right. We didn't even have to send anything to the lab. One of the homicide investigators is the son of a butcher. He said he used to work in the shop, and he knows lamb bones when he sees them."

"Okay, then, I guess it's lamb bones."

Chief Harry could barely contain his amusement. "I

107

hadda agree with him, when he explained what he was talking about. We're obviously dealing with an animal. I told them to let the builders start digging again."

"Okay. Well. Good. Lamb bones. No crime."

"Kinda makes you feel like a fool, don't it?" While Kreevitch tried to decide whether it would do him more good to answer no or yes or to remain silent, Chief Harry added, "Incidentally, we just got a call about a prowler from the lady who lives across the street from your friend Ferryman. She says somebody is creeping around in the old guy's yard. You want to take it?"

"Right."

"If you find any steak bones or like that, I don't want to hear about it, okay?"

"Right."

The granite ball rolled straight at Mother Grey. Like one of those dreams where disaster comes closer and closer while paralysis grips the limbs, she stood there watching it roll, marveling at its remarkable shininess and at the veins in the surface of the stone. "Look out!" everybody shouted again, everybody except Claudine, who was chanting. Just in time she jumped sideways out of the way. The ball rolled on past, somehow not hitting any tombstones, picked up speed, missed Delight van Buskirk by inches, clattered down the long wide flight of steps, bounced off the hood of somebody's car, and hurtled crashing and splintering through the front door of Peter Susswald's house. A howl of distress escaped the bookseller's lips; the door was old, made of solid oak, and he had just had it expensively refinished.

"What was that?" Shannon said.

From over the hill they heard the roaring of engines, the grinding of gears. The thieves were still here. "Be careful," Mother Grey said. "You'd better go back down and stay with the others until the police arrive."

"Why? What was it?"

"A granite ball. Somebody knocked it off its pedestal up at the top of the hill. I think the cemetery thieves are still up there."

"Let's go get 'em, then." Shannon started running.

"Watch out! They're dangerous!" Mother Grey was getting out of breath, running along beside her. Over her shoulder she could see the rest of the Friends following up the hill behind them.

"I'm dangerous too," Shannon said. "I'm trained in martial arts. And I want to see my grandfather's tombstone."

On the shoulder of the driveway between St. Joseph's cemetery and Mount Outlook, a large yellow panel truck started its engine and slowly drove away. There was no other sound except for the ragged panting breaths of the women and the thudding of their feet. Finally they had to stop. Peter Susswald caught up with them.

"Those balls are supposed to be drilled for metal rods to hold them to their pedestals," he said. "They shouldn't come loose that way. Did you see anyone?"

"Only something that looked like a rental truck," Mother Grey said. "Beyond those trees. I heard it start up and drive away just now."

"It must have been the thieves," Shannon said. "I don't suppose anybody here has a cell phone."

Mother Grey shook her head. "Not me." Modern gadgets had no place in her life. She was a Luddite to the core, and besides, there wasn't any money at St. Bede's for such stuff.

"Here's where that ball came from," said Peter. He pointed to a bare pedestal, at whose base was a depression in the earth where the granite sphere had fallen. They could see the track of the ball running downhill through the grass.

Other tracks appeared underneath the trail of the granite ball, the tracks of a small front-end loader. "They went this way," Peter Susswald said, and followed the tracks up beyond some shrubbery, only to find the chain-link fence flattened out and the tracks ending by the roadside. The miserable wretches hadn't even used the gate.

"They must have loaded whatever it was onto a truck and driven the whole thing away," Peter said. "We should call the police right away, before they can get far."

"Mr. Ferryman lives right through the gate," Shannon said. "I'm sure he'll let us use his phone." As Peter and Shannon made for John Ferryman's phone, other Friends came chuffing up the hill and milled around. Even Martine was back. Seeing them all at the upper end of the cemetery, she had driven her car around and parked at the top.

It was Shannon who first reached Mr. Ferryman's house. But she didn't go in. She stood outside, screaming.

"Now what?" said Mother Grey.

"It happened," Claudine said. "I told you." Mother Grey went through the gate and across the road to see what the shouting was about.

Shannon had stopped screaming. Now she was holding her mouth and pointing to the bushes beside the side door to John Ferryman's house. Work boots stuck out from behind them, thick work boots stained with concrete. Someone was lying in the bushes. Taking a look, Mother Grey thought it was John Ferryman himself. Then she thought, *No, his head is the wrong shape.* But his head was the wrong shape for anybody. Or anybody living.

Beside the bushes, the granite back doorstep to John Ferryman's house had been turned over somehow and cast aside, leaving only bugs and mud in front of the door. Standing there with a bloody crowbar in his hand was Mark Smith.

"Shannon, Shannon, stop that," Mark was saying. "Look here. I found it. Right where they said it was. Your friend Ferryman was using it for a doorstep." He was pointing with the crowbar at a slab of granite. Mother Grey now saw that it was a gravestone. Even with the mud, she could see words carved in it: "James Waring Smith, 1923–1955, Lost in the Great Flood. A youth to Fortune and to Fame unknown." Above the lettering was a sailing ship in low relief.

She looked up to see Jack Kreevitch pulling up to the curb in his police cruiser, not using the siren but flashing the lights. The pulsing red shone on people's faces, on Mark Smith's face. Kreevitch got out of the car and approached the knot of people. The radio at his hip buzzed and crackled, startling them out of their stupor, and the crowd parted to let him through.

"See? Look at this," Mark Smith said to Kreevitch. "Remember what I was trying to tell you? This proves it. I hope you understand everything now."

"Explain it to me," Kreevitch said. *There is always*

time to explain, thought Mother Grey. Kreevitch had not seen the body yet.

"John Ferryman killed my father, buried him under the Acme, and stole his tombstone so that he could treat it disrespectfully every day." *Always time to explain, although the explanations may not always make sense.*

Then Kreevitch noticed John Ferryman lying in the bushes. He knelt down and felt for a pulse in the old man's neck.

"He's gone, isn't he?" Mother Grey said.

"Yep," Kreevitch said. " 'Fraid he didn't make it."

"Make what?" Mark Smith said.

Shannon said, "He's dead, Daddy."

"Who?" Mark Smith turned around and, as though for the first time, looked into the bushes. "What? Who's that?"

"I think it used to be John Ferryman," Kreevitch said.

It took Mark Smith a moment to decide how to react to this, and when he did, it was to strike an attitude of bravado. "Good. I'm glad to hear it. The son of a bitch should have died before he met my mother." He looked at the crowbar in his hand, noticed the blood, and dropped it like a snake. "This was all bloody before, by the way."

"So," Kreevitch said. He took out the handcuffs. "You decided this man had murdered your father forty years ago, and so you struck him with the crowbar and killed him in revenge. Is that right?"

"No, I didn't," Mark said.

"Maybe you didn't really mean to hurt him."

"I didn't even see him."

"Mr. Smith, I wonder if you'd mind coming down to the station with me to answer a few questions."

"I didn't do anything to him! I came up here, and the crowbar was lying on the step."

"Put your hands behind your back please, sir. You have the right to remain silent."

"Honey, tell them. Tell them the crowbar was there already. Tell them about the phone call, the reason I came up here."

"The phone call?" Shannon said.

"The phone call, the phone call. A man rang up my hotel room and said to come up here and look at John Ferryman's back doorstep if I wanted to know what happened to my father's tombstone." He was wiggling his wrists. "That's too tight."

"Just bear with me awhile, sir. We'll take them off when we get to the station," Kreevitch said. As he propelled Mark Smith toward the cruiser, he glanced around at the crowd. Some of them were frowning and muttering. Mother Grey could tell he was wishing for backup; a mob, even a mob of sprout-eating tree huggers, as Kreevitch liked to call them, could turn ugly in a moment. If he said it once, he said it a hundred times; It was a mistake to send officers into these situations alone. Only a month ago he had been telling Mother Grey how he had responded to a call about a simple domestic dispute, only to have the wife and five of the children jump all over him and try to steal his club and his radio.

Even in Fishersville these things happened. Police officers should go in pairs, he always said.

"Daddy, I wasn't there."

The way nuns did.

"All right, you weren't in the room. But I told you about it."

"No, I—"

"I'm not saying anything more without an attorney."
He cast a meaningful glance at Kreevitch.

"Right," Kreevitch said, pushing his head down as he
stuffed him into the car. "You have the right to remain
silent, you have the right to an attorney. . . ."

"What's going on?" Martine Wellworth whispered to
Mother Grey. Mother Grey spread her hands, the gesture
taking in the dead body, the prisoner in the car, the dis-
traught daughter, the whole picture.

"I would say he needs an attorney," Martine said.

"I would say so too. His name is Mark Smith," said
Mother Grey. "He comes from Phoenix, Arizona. He can
probably even afford to pay you. Go for it." While Martine went for it, Mother Grey madly photographed the
crime scene, including as many of the bystanders as she
could before they could get away. Hey, you never knew.
Maybe the murderer himself was in that crowd somewhere.

"Mother Vinnie, what are you doing?" Jack said. He
was putting crime scene tape around the bushes, and the
roll was running out.

"Nothing. Taking pictures."

"Quit it."

"I didn't step on anything."

"Go home." Other police cars began to arrive.

"All right. Do you want to see these when I get them
developed?"

"No. Yes. Get them to make me an extra set of
prints."

"Two extra sets, Jack," she said. "One for Martine."
He stood glaring at her, his hands on his hips, blocking
the space between two shrubs where the crime scene
tape had run out. Then Peter Susswald came out of the

cemetery and engaged him in conversation, and she was able to take a few more shots without Kreevitch shouting at her.

"I hate to bother you with the trivial problems of the Mount Outlook Cemetery," Peter said, "with a murder on your hands and all, but the graveyard was robbed this afternoon. I have here a list of all the graveyard ornaments." He brandished his notebook at Kreevitch. "If you'd like me to, I can check to see how many of these are missing."

"Cross off the gravestone with the ship carving," Mother Grey called to him. "We seem to have found it." He crossed it off. She photographed the stone again from a slightly different angle. Meanwhile Martine Wellworth puttered around taking notes, preparing her case for the defense. If it came to that, she said later. No reason why his case should ever come to trial. The evidence was all circumstantial.

The council of war took place around Mother Grey's kitchen table, just like old times. Shannon was a basket case and needed therapy from both animals to keep her calm enough to remain seated. Scratch occupied her lap, kneading her sweater and drooling, while Towser rested his chin on her instep and thumped his tail.

First they had to have lunch, strong drafts of tea and peanut butter sandwiches. Two of the three sets of photos Mother Grey got done at the one-hour KwickiePik were spread out on the table as soon as the women had choked the last morsel down.

Martine had made piles of notes. " 'A youth to Fortune and to Fame unknown,' " she read.

Mother Grey knew the rest of the quote. "'Fair Science frown'd not on his humble birth, and Melancholy mark'd him for her own,'" she said. "It's from Gray's 'Elegy.' Shannon's great-grandmother Smith must have been fond of poetry."

Shannon left off petting the cat and stared into space. "I saw him spit on it," she murmured. "I think he must have spit and wiped his feet on it every day for forty years."

"What? The gravestone?" Mother Grey was horrified.

"Mr. Ferryman hated my grandfather."

"I guess he must have."

"This can't be happening. Why didn't I let my dad leave town when he wanted to?"

"Just between us," said Martine, "do you think your father capable of killing Mr. Ferryman?" It was something to consider. Mark Smith was a stranger in Fishersville and clearly unhinged. Nobody here knew what he might be capable of. People killed other people all the time, got off on technicalities, moved to other towns, and did it again. The people in the new town were always astonished. Trainloads of migratory murderers could be roaming all over the state of New Jersey and points beyond, stab, choke, hey taxi. A story in the paper just last month told of a wife-murderer who had escaped justice in another state and settled in Freehold or someplace, where he had started a whole new family, only to end up whacking the second wife.

"I don't know what to think," said Shannon, as though reading Mother Grey's bleak thoughts. "He's never done anything like this before. Not even remotely. But he isn't well. Can either of you recommend a good psychiatrist?"

They discussed the concept of a good psychiatrist for a while, agreeing finally that a good psychiatrist for Mark would be one who not only would appear in court to represent his state of mind in the most advantageous light, but who would also help him clinically. Shannon kept saying that her father was out of his mind, and Martine kept shushing her.

"Say rather that he's upset." She promised to make some calls Monday until she found a competent doctor who would agree to go and interview Mark Smith in the county jail.

"Your father didn't kill Mr. Ferryman," Mother Grey said. "At least he didn't do what Jack Kreevitch seems to think: turn over the back step, discover the gravestone, fly into a rage, and beat Mr. Ferryman with the crowbar, in that order."

"How do you know?" said Shannon.

She held out the snapshot of the gravestone. "Because of the blood."

"Right," said Martine. "See that? There's blood on the gravestone where it was pried with the crowbar. So the crowbar had to have been used as a weapon before it was used as a tool."

Shannon wasn't sure. "The blood could have just dripped on the gravestone after Mr. Ferryman was killed."

"No," Mother Grey said. "That isn't a drip."

Anyway, Martine said, it was enough to create reasonable doubt in the mind of a jury, which was what she seemed to feel was important.

"Take a look at these, Shannon," said Mother Grey. "See whether anything about them strikes you." She kept out the pictures that showed the body; Shannon had been fond of the old man.

"Who do you think did kill him, then?" Shannon asked. The question was probably rhetorical, but Martine answered, "Some other enemy."

"One of the cemetery thieves," Mother Grey suggested.

"Why kill him? Why not just . . ."

"He was headed back to his house to call the police."

"We were going to call the police too. Nobody killed us," Shannon said.

"Not because they didn't try. Someone nearly used me for a bowling pin." In her mind's eye Mother Grey saw it again, the monstrous shiny ball cannoning toward her. Paralytic terror was a new experience, a sign of middle age perhaps. Next year she would be forty. The faculties departed, one by one, with the advancing years, they said; maybe the first to go was the ability to jump out of the way of rolling death.

"Still. To stop and kill him, rather than just run away." Shannon looked at the pictures of the people in the crowd. "Maybe he saw their faces," she said.

"Ah," said Mother Grey.

"Maybe he recognized them from somewhere. Maybe he knew them," Shannon said.

"You think the graveyard was robbed by somebody Mr. Ferryman knew?" Martine said.

"It could have happened that way," Shannon said. "He saw them taking things, and he was going back to call the police, so whoever it was followed him and killed him."

"Who would he know that would do such a thing?" Mother Grey said.

"His son," Shannon said.

"What?" Martine said.

"Who?" Mother Grey said.

"He has this son. I think he just got out of jail or something. Maybe he did it."

Perhaps John Ferryman had been done to death by his own son. No doubt he was capable of it. In Mother Grey's opinion, anyone who would sleep in a crypt and then go away and leave a perfectly good camping kit was capable of any sort of deranged act.

But Martine was not convinced. "Mention it to Officer Kreevitch, if you like," she said to Shannon, "but don't be surprised if he doesn't put out an immediate APB."

"You think he won't believe me."

"He'll need a lot more evidence to persuade him your dad didn't do it. You remember how bad it looked for him." Mother Grey was sorry Martine had said that, because Shannon did remember how bad it looked, having seen for herself, and now that Martine had reminded her, she began to shiver and shake again. What the girl needed was some sort of distraction.

"I've got to go," Martine said. She had to relieve Albert, who had things he would rather be doing on a Saturday afternoon than watching little Henry. She promised to get Mark a shrink by Monday, wished them good luck, and departed.

Maybe it would relax Shannon to go and see another nice motherly old lady. Mabel Weeds, the old friend of Nana's, was expecting them to come calling. Something to show them, she had said she had.

10

The thing that Mrs. Weeds wanted to show them proved to be a stack of six or seven letters, tied up in a ribbon, still in their yellowed envelopes, addressed in an old-fashioned hand to Mrs. Francis Weeds. After the welcome, after the cookies and tea, after a brief spate of small talk, Mrs. Weeds produced the packet from a desk drawer and handed it solemnly to Mother Grey. The package felt light for a thing of such gravity; it was as though the old lady had given her the dead body of a small animal, a mouse, say, or a songbird.

"That's Nana's writing," Shannon said.

"Yes, dear. Your grandmother sent me these letters soon after she moved to Phoenix. I've kept them ever since, because . . . well, just because I always keep things." Clearly this was true. Mrs. Weeds's house was

cluttered with the things she kept: newspapers, maga-
zines, bills, books, crochet projects, sweepstakes offers,
knitted afghans, half-empty cookie boxes, footstools, an-
timacassars, cats.

Shannon took the letters from Mother Grey and sat
staring at them, almost as though she expected the letters themselves to make the next move, to speak to her
even, and to say something that she wasn't yet prepared
to hear.

"Read them," Mrs. Weeds said. "Go ahead. If you
want to, you can have them to keep. But there's a story
that goes with them, and you have to hear it if you want
to understand what those letters were all about."

Slowly Shannon undid the narrow peach-colored ribbon, drew out the first of the letters, and began to read.

Mother Grey sipped her tea. Shannon giggled. "How
funny to hear her call Dad 'little Markie,'" she said, and
kept on reading. After a while she looked up. "What does
she mean, grateful to you and Father John for saying
nothing? Saying nothing about what?"

"Jim Smith—well, read the other letters, dear. You'll
understand."

Shannon took the next letter out of its envelope, read
a bit of it, and looked up again, her face clouding. "What
does she mean, 'a relief to hear that Jim didn't somehow
show up for his own memorial service'? Why would he
show up? He was dead, wasn't he?"

"We never knew for certain," said Mrs. Weeds. Interesting. So that was the dark secret, that Jim Smith (the
sales engineer, that is, not the airline pilot or the dog
trainer) might still be alive.

"And why a relief?" Shannon asked.

"That's the story I have to tell you."

"Oh, this is so sad," Shannon said. "Listen to this, Mother Grey. She writes, 'I still think of John Ferryman and the opportunity I threw away for a decent life. I hope he still thinks of me. If things work out, I mean to come back to him.'"

"He thought of her right up to the hour of his death," Mother Grey said. "Why didn't she ever come back?"

"She stayed away for shame," Mrs. Weeds said.

"Shame?" Shannon might never have heard the word. Indeed, Mother Grey reflected, shame was an antiquated concept these days, when people could appear on television and boast of ruining their lives.

Mrs. Weeds explained shame to Shannon: "If someone did a woman an injury years ago, it reflected badly on her. If you married an unsuitable man, people didn't feel sorry for you for making a mistake, but scornful. Nobody exposed their wounds to public view, because if you were wounded, you must be incompetent. People would try to hide that. It wasn't like it is today."

"I see," Shannon said.

"Young people today have no idea how shame could shrivel a woman, paralyze her, until she couldn't take the smallest step in public."

"But what was Mary Agnes's shame?" Mother Grey asked.

"How she was deceived by Jim Smith."

"What did he do?" Shannon asked.

Mabel Weeds took her linen napkin in her hands and pleated it carefully, folding down the pleats and pressing them between her fingers. "There was another woman."

"He had an affair, and for this she drove him out of the house to his death in the raging flood? That sounds kind of harsh," Shannon said.

"Wait. It wasn't like that. Let me tell you the whole thing. This other woman lived across the river in Pennsylvania, in another town. Your grandfather traveled for a living, you know, so he could be away for long periods of time without anyone suspecting. He kept the woman in the other house for years and years."

"But Nana found out about her somehow," Shannon said.

"Yes." Mrs. Weeds put down her teacup, sighed a long quavering sigh, and began to stroke one of her cats. "It was his birthday, you see. Mary Agnes and Mark had a little cake for him after supper. Her parents came over. You never knew your great-grandmother Fitzroy, dear; she died before you were born. But she was a sweet person.

"After he had eaten his piece of cake, Jim Smith jumped up from the table and said he had to leave; he had business in Harrisburg the next day. His mother-in-law said, 'Are you going to drive all night?' and he said, 'Don't worry, Mother Fitzroy, I'll be safe. I'll drink lots of coffee.' "

"He kissed his mother-in-law, and then his wife; he tousled his little boy's hair, she told me; and then he went out.

"But this time Mary Agnes was suspicious. After all these years, something finally suggested to her that Jim Smith's life was not what it seemed."

"What made her suspicious?" Shannon asked.

"I never asked her. I think it was something intimate.

"We had arranged beforehand that she would borrow my car and follow after him the next time he left on one of his journeys, to see where he might be going. I lived next door to her then, in that brick house where the Burgesses are living now. It was a simple matter for Mary Agnes to run over and get my keys and then follow him across the bridge and into Pennsylvania. I had already promised to look after Markie while she was gone."

"So where did he go?" said Shannon.

"He drove and drove, and she followed along behind him, staying just out of his sight, far, far out into the country. After almost an hour of driving, turning this way and that on big highways and small, he turned into a long driveway leading up to a house on a hill. Every light in the house was burning. A big party was going on. Crowds of people were walking up the steps and going in."

"I can just see them," Shannon said, "all in furs and cloche hats, streaming into the brightly lit house, and in the darkness Nana coming closer and closer, with the fog swirling around her feet, just like the last scene of *Gone With the Wind*."

"I don't know about fog and furs—it was the middle of August, after all—but they would have been wearing nice summer dresses, and the men in suits. Cloche hats weren't popular, either, in 1955. Although there was a kind of hat with no crown and a turned-down brim that stuck out over our faces, like a big soup plate—mine was trimmed with white marabou feathers—"

"No furs, then," said Mother Grey, wanting her to dispense with the frills and get on to the meat of the story.

But Mrs. Weeds was inclined to play along with Shannon, finding the romance of it. "I suppose they wore those dresses with the full skirts and tiny waists," she said, "that were so stylish in 1955. Some of them even came in limousines with chauffeurs, Mary Agnes said. It was a hot night. They smelled of Arpège and Chanel Number Five, clouds of expensive perfume all around the house. Nobody noticed Mary Agnes coming up the driveway behind Jim Smith, because there were so many people there already."

"A huge stylish party," Mother Grey said. "Please go on."

"Mary Agnes went to the front door, and a maid was letting people in. A maid! And Mary Agnes and Markie living in that hovel on Water Street!"

"What did she do?"

"She said, 'Please tell Mr. Smith that Mrs. Smith is here.' Mary Agnes wanted to be civilized about the whole thing. You always want to try to be civilized for as long as you can. But as soon as she saw his face, with the Fräulein, or perhaps I should say the Frau, hanging on his arm, she just lost all control."

"They were married?" Shannon said.

"Everyone there seemed to regard them as married."

"And the other woman was German?"

Mrs. Weeds shrugged. "German, Austrian, Swiss. Her name was Gerta or Katrina or something like that." She went on to describe how Jim Smith's other family appeared in the archway in a touching tableau: the Fräulein/Frau, her golden braids coiled around her head; the three children, a boy and two little girls, clustered around her knees. In her mind Mother Grey pictured the von Trapps all in a line.

"People were dancing," Mrs. Weeds went on, as if that fact by itself constituted the final outrage. "The party was another birthday party, you see, for Jim Smith. There was a band."

"A big band?" Shannon said. "Like Tommy Dorsey or Duke Ellington?"

"No, just three pieces, I think, a piano, drums, and one saxophone or something like that. Next you'll be asking me what music they were playing. I'm sorry, dear, I don't know. I wasn't there."

"But there was a cake, with candles on it," Shannon prompted.

"A cake, yes, and fifty or sixty guests. Who could have known that Jim Smith had so many friends in his other life?"

Then suddenly Shannon saw the true shape and color of the story. "My grandfather was a bigamist."

"Yes. A bigamist. Jim Smith was maintaining two households, and that of Mary Agnes was not the best kept."

"What did she do when she realized all this?" said Mother Grey.

"She lost her temper."

"She called him dirty names," said Shannon.

"No, women didn't use foul language in 1955 unless they were very badly brought up," Mrs. Weeds said. "And Mary Agnes was never that, but she did tell me she shouted at him. She told him she never wanted to see him again, that she was going to tell everyone in Fishersville that he had died, including Markie, and if he ever showed his face in town again, she was going to see that he got put in jail for bigamy."

"And what was the German wife doing while all this shouting was going on? Just standing there?" Mother Grey asked.

"Yes, just standing there staring at Mary Agnes, with her children grabbing her around the knees. I've no idea what she thought. Maybe she didn't understand enough English to know what was going on. Anyway, Mary Agnes got back in my car and returned to Fishersville."

"And that was the last she saw of him?" Shannon said.

"Oh, no, no. He followed her home."

"Why?"

"Would you believe it? He refused to accept that their so-called marriage was over. He came back. He said he had discussed it with the German woman, and she had told him he'd never get rid of either one of them."

"My word."

"Walked right into their bedroom and took off his pants, she told me. 'Move over, honey, I'm home,' he said, or words to that effect."

Gossip. Mother Grey was breathless with curiosity, in spite of herself. "What did she do then?"

"Whatever she did, or said, it caused him to throw a terrible tantrum. I don't think he expected her to stick up for herself."

"He hit her?" Shannon said.

"No. She thought he was going to hit her, but instead he punched his fist through the window and cut himself on the arm, a very bad cut all the way from his hand to his elbow. She thought he would bleed to death right in front of her, and God help her, she didn't care, she told me. In fact, she was never sure whether he hadn't actually bled to death from the cut after he took Archie's boat and set out across the water."

"So all of this happened the night of the flood," Shannon said.

"Yes, didn't I mention that? After Jim Smith got back to Fishersville, the water rose so high that the bridge had to be closed, and he couldn't drive his car back to Pennsylvania. That was why he took the boat. Between the flood waters and his wounded arm, we never knew for certain whether he got swept over the wing dam and drowned, or survived somehow and went back to his other home in Radderford."

"Mary Agnes never told this story to her parents?"

"Not even to her parents. Only to me."

For a long time they sat in silence, broken only by the purring of cats.

"My poor father is a bastard," Shannon said finally.

"How so?" Mother Grey said.

"His father's marriage to his mother wasn't valid."

"We don't know that."

"We do. Father Angleford did. There was a line drawn through the entry in his records that said they were married. I wondered about that when I saw it."

"You don't have to tell your father about it," Mrs. Weeds said. "I don't plan to. Besides, this is the nineties. Nobody cares about issues of legitimacy anymore."

"Somehow," Shannon said, "I think he would care."

Mother Grey thought so too, unstable as he was, sensitive to the smallest slight, even paranoid. But where did John Ferryman fit into this tale? How was it that, being legally free, she never married him? "I take it that Mary Agnes never returned to his other house to see whether he had survived the flood," Mother Grey said.

"Never," Mrs. Weeds said. "As far as she was concerned, he was dead."

"Radderford," said Shannon. "Did she ever tell you where it was, the house she followed him to?"

"No, just somewhere around Radderford. I tried to track him down once, even though she made me promise not to, because she was having a hard time in Phoenix and needed money. He really should have helped her and their son. But since she never told me the exact address in Radderford and since every other man in that town seems to be called Jim Smith, I had to give it up."

"What about the car he drove to Fishersville?" Mother Grey said. "Did anybody come to claim it?"

"Mary Agnes drove it to Phoenix and kept it. Nobody ever came after her to take it back. I myself think it was the least she was entitled to."

"So Jim Smith might have been dead after all," Mother Grey said.

"By this time he probably is," Mrs. Weeds said. "After all, more than forty years have gone by."

"But she wrote to you that she was planning to come back to John Ferryman," Shannon said, holding her tote bag and rocking.

"Ah," Mrs. Weeds said. "That's another story."

"She met another man," Mother Grey guessed.

"She met Mr. C," Mrs. Weeds said. "After that it was all over for her with men."

"Mr. C?"

"Breast cancer. She had the mastectomy, you see, and she never felt right about herself again."

"Oh, yes, that," said Shannon.

"Then too she was paying off her medical bills for some years afterward and hadn't the money to travel," Mrs. Weeds said. "And after a certain amount of time went by, John Ferryman gave up on her and married Penny."

"My word," Mother Grey said.

"John was married twice, you know. His first wife

was Yvonne. That was Ronnie's mother. She ran away and left them."

"Married twice?" Shannon said. "I thought he loved Nana."

"He did. But no man will wait forever." She looked at Mother Grey, with that uncanny ability the old sometimes have of seeing into the hearts of others. "If you find the one for you," she said, "you must take him and hold on to him. No matter what people might say."

She means Dave Dogg, Mother Grey thought. Or maybe she didn't mean anything. Maybe it was just a random shot. Mrs. Weeds picked up her teacup again. Surely the tea was cold by now. Shannon hugged her tote bag and rested her cheek against it. Mother Grey thought, yes, what a comfort it would be to find the one for her, take him, and hold on to him. And how unacceptable it would be to share him. What was it Jack Kreevitch had heard about Felicia? Maybe she had been run over by a beer truck. Maybe Dave wanted to come back. Well, what if he did come back? But what would people say? On the other hand, would she truly care what people said?

A fruitless line of inquiry. Shannon was reading the letters again, one by one, and passing them to Mother Grey when she was finished. Mother Grey turned her attention to the letters and away from what her best friend was pleased to call her atrophied love life.

One mystery was solved. And yet. The situation with Grandfather Smith was as murky as ever. Did he actually die in the flood? Or might he not have been waylaid by John Ferryman and made away with under cover of the disaster? True, the bones found under the Acme were

131

lamb bones, but as Mark had suggested, they might not be the only bones buried there.

It seemed to Mother Grey that the German woman would have come to Fishersville to find her husband if he didn't come home to her again, particularly if she had really told him, "You'll never get rid of either one of us." But who knew, after all this time, what the woman had really said, or what had happened? Think of those four people in Delio's, eyewitnesses, they said, who gave four completely different stories of the events of the night of the flood.

"There's only one way to find out," Shannon said. "We'll go to Radderford and find my grandfather's other family, if they're still there. Whether he's dead or alive, I have to know what happened."

"Right now?" said Mrs. Weeds.

"Right now," Shannon said. "What do you say, Mother Vinnie?"

Tomorrow was Sunday, but everything at St. Bede's had been prepared, and she could always wing the homily; it wouldn't be the first time, or the last. "Let's go," she said. "Thank you so much for the tea, Mrs. Weeds."

They stopped at the rectory first, because Towser had to be walked and Mother Grey wanted to pick up the things one needs for a longish car trip. When they came back in from walking the dog, there was a new message from Dave on the answering machine.

"We have to stop playing telephone tag, Vinnie. I'll be here by the phone tonight at seven o'clock. If you don't call me, then I'm coming over." Then a beep and a click.

"Who's that? Your boyfriend?"

"Priests don't have boyfriends," said Mother Grey.

What an undignified term. Call him my main squeeze. Former. My former main squeeze.

"He sounded frantic. Didn't you think so?" Shannon said.

"Did he?" She dialed his number, but it was busy. "I guess talking to Dave will have to keep," she said. "Let's go."

"Are you sure? At seven tonight we'll probably still be in Radderford," Shannon said. "Don't you want to wait and try to get him?"

"No, I want to go now," Mother Grey said. "He's probably on the Internet or something. He could be hours. I'll have to call him tomorrow and find out what he wants to talk about." Actually she didn't want to talk to him.

Shannon looked her in the eye, penetrating the careful mask of indifference. "You're in love with him, aren't you? I bet he's in love with you. Are you star-crossed?"

Mother Grey wasn't ready to talk to him right now, to hear his voice actually responding to her. It must have been, oh, a month and a half after he turned his back on her that she stopped saying to herself, *If only Dave were here*, seven or eight times a day; she was able to cut down to three times, and then two, and now she hardly ever thought of him except when it was time to go to sleep and just before breakfast. If she talked to him over the phone, maybe they would start up again. "We must be star-crossed," she said. Dave would have other words for it, rude words, the sort of words that customarily formed the vocabulary of an inner-city policeman, but *star-crossed* worked as well as anything.

"I love the sound of his voice," Shannon said. "It's intensely romantic."

"Romantic as in painful," Mother Grey said. "Are you thinking of your grandmother's stories again?"

"Her stories were very beautiful."

"My life is very beautiful, and I live it all by myself, just me and the Lord. And my cello. And my cat. And my little dog Towser."

"Nobody can live without true love," Shannon said.

11

When at last they rolled into Radderford, their first stop was a big newsstand with a public phone. The local telephone directory was on a stand next to it, anchored to aluminum covers. Much wear and tear had been inflicted on the directory, and some of the yellowing pages were torn out altogether, but the three pages of Smiths remained intact. Surely one of them would be a man of seventy-odd years named James Waring Smith.

"There are fourteen J. Smiths in Radderford," Shannon pointed out, "and five Smiths named James."

"Good," Mother Grey said. "Write down the addresses of all of them, and we'll cruise around the streets of Radderford scoping them out. When we see one we like, we'll stop." She bought a Hagstrom map of the county. The streets were laid out in minute detail, with indications of street numbers. Then she bought a fat yellow marker.

"We're going to need more gas than we have," Shannon said. The tank was half full, which should be plenty, inasmuch as Mother Grey was praying for a revelation from the Holy Spirit, the force that upheld and sustained her in times of stress and also sometimes gave her handy tips. Plenty. If he were still alive and living in Radderford, the right Jim Smith's house would send out some signal to them long before they ran out of gas.

But just in case the house took longer to find than Mother Grey was expecting, they stopped and filled the tank.

Several of the J. Smiths lived on a long street in the middle of town, and three in a single block, which proved to be composed of apartments and row houses. They decided to tackle these first. The first address on their list was one of the row houses, up a long flight of steps. No one was home.

The second door they knocked on, farther down the street, was opened by a merry and pleasant young man who joshed them and flirted with Shannon. His name, he said, was Jamaal Smith. He was clearly not related by blood to the fair-skinned Irish Smiths, being a very dark-skinned African-American. He knew of no James W. Smith. No one answered at the third address. At the fourth try the door was opened by another African-American, about a hundred years old, whose name, he said, was Jeremiah. Jeremiah was very cranky. They had awakened him from his nap. He sent them away unsatisfied.

A few blocks down the street they found Jennifer, who was white but female, no relation to a Jim Smith, she said. Then in another part of town they raised a fellow who was white, male, and actually named James but was too young to be anybody's grandfather.

And so the afternoon progressed, through failure after failure. "I'm beginning to think we may not find him," Shannon said.

"The trail is very cold," Mother Grey agreed. "But take heart." Something about the thirteenth house of Smith called out to her. "Try this one."

Shannon pulled the rental car over to the curb and got out in front of a small bungalow with ivy growing up the side of the porch. The inhabitants were surely of the right generation; a white 1979 Mercury Monarch sat in the driveway, an old man's car if ever there was one, and the hedges and lawn seemed to belong to someone who was too old and tired for yard work.

Sure enough, the householder was sitting and rocking on the porch behind the ivy, smoking a pipe and reading the newspaper. A television grandfather, a grandfather to die for, with cheeks like apples and wrinkles that were all made out of laugh lines.

"Hi," said Shannon. "I'm looking for a Mr. James Smith."

The old man looked up from his reading. "That would be me," he said. "What can I do for you? You wouldn't be from those sweepstakes people, would you?"

"No, no. I'm Shannon Smith. I don't quite know how to say this, but I'm here to find my grandfather, James W. Smith, who disappeared from Fishersville, New Jersey, during the great flood of 1955."

He got up from the chair, stiffly, and gave her a smile that spread in crinkles all over his face. "Wish I could say it was me," he said. "All my grandchildren have gone to California. I've never been in Fishersville."

Shannon's face fell. "Are you sure?" she said. "Think. Nineteen fifty-five was a long time ago. Maybe you've forgotten."

"I'm not even James W. Smith," he said. "I'm James C. Would you ladies like some iced tea? I can have my wife fix you something."

"No, thank you," Shannon said. "Gee, I wish—oh, well."

"There is a James W. Smith living in that big place behind the stone wall out on the Old York Road. Have you tried him?"

"No."

"I would have thought you'd try him first, if you thought you might be related. He's the richest man in town." He chuckled, took a pull on his pipe, and gave them detailed directions.

The house the old man had directed them to bore no resemblance to the place in Mary Agnes's story, at least none to the place Shannon had imagined. Far from being on a lonely country road, it was on a heavily trafficked highway, big trucks, concrete mixers, and semis roaring along with blinding speed and deafening noise. Perhaps the surrounding acreage had been rolling fields and woods once, even as recently as five years ago, but now they were crowded with new houses, some with people living in them and some still under construction. On the crossroads that had once been so lonely stood an enormous shopping center with two grocery chains, a pizzeria, and a clothing store called Today's Man.

Nevertheless this was the traffic light the old man

had described. Beyond the intersection, as he had promised, they saw the J. W. Smith house.

The high stone wall was covered with vines. Stone lions crouched on either side of the gate, and beyond the gate Shannon and Mother Grey could see the house, imposing under ancient trees.

Shannon thought it somehow an intellectual house. She pictured her grandfather in his study, maybe wearing a smoking jacket. In her daydream he closed the leather-bound book he was reading and stared out the window, brushing a stray white hair from his noble (if wrinkled) brow, his thoughts straying to his real family, lost ever since the flood so many years ago, and all because of . . . what? His tragic case of amnesia? His wicked German mistress, who controlled his mind against his will? Shannon's solitary-regret fantasy evaporated as she saw that he had company today; expensive cars were parked all over the lawn, and the people getting out of them and trooping up the porch steps were festively dressed in flowered prints and laces.

A party. Shannon experienced an instant of déjà vu, like a rabbit walking over her grave. Or was the rabbit image a cliché? *Who knows what it's like when a rabbit walks on your grave? Probably it's not like anything. Probably it wouldn't make any more impression than a rabbit walking anywhere else.* And anyway Shannon didn't have a grave; she was alive. Okay, it was like being Nana, reliving her bad time. But maybe this wasn't the place where all that happened. It could still be some other Jim Smith. She put her hand in the tote bag and touched the box of ashes.

The grounds were beautifully kept. In the distance

they could see gardeners in brown coveralls puttering about with hedge clippers and rakes.

"What a pile," said Mother Grey. "If this is where your grandfather lives, he must be rich as Croesus."

"This can't be my grandfather's house," Shannon said.

"What do you suppose is going on? Maybe it's a wedding," Mother Grey said. "Look, there's a caterer's truck. And see the tent in back."

"At least we can get something to eat," Shannon said. "We'll pretend we're friends of the groom." She did a mental check of her habiliments and decided that she could pass for a wedding guest, if nobody noticed the wooden clogs on her feet; she was wearing a dress, after all, and even some purple eye shadow, and of course Mother Grey had on her collar and dark suit, appropriate for any occasion.

The rental car slipped between the lions, up the drive, and into a parking place between a black Infiniti and a bright red Jaguar XK8. "A party," she muttered. Mother Grey did little grooming things, patting her hair, smoothing her skirt with her hands.

"We'll go in only for a minute," Mother Grey said. "Just long enough to find out whether this is the right place." Shannon was pleased to notice that her car, polished and new, was not conspicuous among these fancy cars.

"First the caterer's tent," Shannon said. "I'm really hungry."

"Good plan," Mother Grey said. "We can discreetly pump the caterers about James W. Smith. They won't notice we're strangers here." But the yellow tent was harder to get to than they thought.

The way the gardens were arranged, it was necessary to go in the front way, through the house, to get to the food tent out back. Making believe they were guests, Shannon and Mother Grey joined the stream going up the porch steps and in the front door. In her bare legs and wooden clogs and gripping her bookstore tote bag, Shannon felt for a moment like a character in one of the fairy tales Nana used to read to her before she went to sleep. *Softly Princess Shannon crept into the castle of the usurper queen, disguised as a humble pig maiden.* Well, as softly as you can in wooden clogs.

The inside of the house seemed even bigger than the outside and looked even more like a castle. On the walls hung oil paintings, originals and not prints, Shannon noted, in heavy gold frames, depicting landscapes and bowls of flowers. Real flowers, beautifully arranged, bedecked the surfaces of tables and mantels.

Above the pocket doors between the living room and the dining room, a string of gold-foil-and-cardboard letters spelled out "Happy Anniversary, Mom and Dad."

"Not a wedding," Shannon observed.

"Never mind. Behave as though you belonged here, and we'll just . . . How *are* you?" Mother Grey smiled and shook the hand of a strange woman accosting her in the hall. "Wonderful to see you."

"Wonderful to see you again," said the strange woman, who had clearly mistaken Mother Grey for someone else. "And this must be your—"

"This is Shannon." Mother Grey beamed.

"I'm so happy for both of you," the woman said. "And how is dear Bishop Spong?"

"The bishop is very well, thank you," Mother Grey said. "Looking forward to his retirement. Please excuse me, I must— Come along, my dear." She took Shannon by the hand and pulled her through the press and out onto the terrace, circumventing some sort of reception line. "She's mistaken me for someone from the Diocese of Newark," she whispered. "I wonder if we'll meet her here."

Beyond the terrace was a garden, lovely in its early spring flowers, pleasing in its layout and proportions, adorned with benches, planters, and fence rails of great charm and respectable antiquity.

It was crowded there as well. Caterer's helpers in white and black passed among the guests, offering them drinks and hors d'oeuvres. Everyone was so oddly welcoming that Shannon began to wonder just who it was that Mother Grey had been mistaken for. Her stomach growled; she edged toward the hot buffet.

As for Mother Grey, she was forced to stop and stave off the conversational onslaughts of a well-oiled guest, a red-faced man with a dusting of white hair. Something she said must have made him realize his mistake:

"I'm sorry. Aren't you Wilhelmine Smith?"

"A colleague," Mother Grey replied.

"Good heavens. How many of you are there?"

"How many of me what?" The question was too much for him; he excused himself and moved on, perhaps to seek another drink. She went to the tent to pump the caterers.

"Mr. Smith has lived here as long as I can remember," said the caterer, as he shaved another slice from the roast beef. Mother Grey thought, *Well then, maybe this is the right house.* "My mother used to work for him when our family first came to Radderford from the old country," he said.

"How long ago was that?" Mother Grey asked.

"Nineteen fifty-six. My mother and father came through the barbed wire, and my brother too. But I was born here."

Mother Grey was not yet born in 1956 and had no idea what went on in the world then. "Which old country was that?" she asked him. Ireland, maybe. He looked Irish. She could see it, the mother with her head scarf and tweed skirt, the brother with his woolly shorts and knee socks, scraping his little pink knees on the cruel barbed wire of the Sassenach.

"Hungary," he said. "It was the year the Russians sent the tanks in."

"What were the Smiths like to work for?"

"All right, I guess. My mother never complained much. Mr. Smith was always nice to her, I think, but the wife was a little—" As another guest approached, or perhaps a family member, his face went blank, instantly becoming a mask of catererly professionalism. "Would you care for one slice or two?" he said.

Mother Grey took her food and went to find Shannon.

The walls and hedges of the grounds held many surprising nooks and alcoves. Shannon found a cubbyhole in the hedge that offered complete privacy, even in the midst of a big party, and there she sat down on a stone bench and began nibbling her supper. Her head boiled with thoughts of meeting her grandfather, and her stomach did too; it was hard to eat. Behind the hedge she gradually became aware of a *snick snick snick* sound in the bushes. Someone was clipping the hedge.

She got up and looked behind her. Afterward she could never tell why. Maybe it was the feeling of eyes boring into her neck; maybe it was the prompting of some evil spirit she had picked up in the cemetery from not wearing Claudine's herbs and crystals, tagging along with her corporeal being to see how much harm it could do.

She looked right into his face. Yes, it was him, John Ferryman's son dressed as a groundskeeper. He smirked at her as if to say "You've seen me naked." *Actually I haven't,* she thought. *I didn't look.*

Mother Grey came and sat down next to her, carrying a plate piled high with ham, roast beef, salad, and delicate little rolls. "This looks very good," she said. "I'm sure they'll never miss it. As soon as I've eaten, we'll go in search of— What is it?"

"That gardener," she whispered. "The one with the hedge clippers."

"Where?"

"He was here a minute ago. It's John Ferryman's son."

"Are you sure?"

"Of course I'm sure. He looked at me. He smiled at me, sort of."

Mother Grey stood up, took a quick look, and turned her head away. "You're right," she said. "It's the cemetery squatter. I still have his sleeping bag. Did you speak to him? What's he doing here?"

"He's doing the hedge, I think. No, I didn't speak to him. I'm scared to death of him."

"Did he speak to you?"

"No."

"Maybe he didn't recognize you. Men smile at pretty girls all the time."

That could be. But no, there was something excessively familiar about the look he had given her, insolent, nasty. Shannon whispered, "I don't think that was it. What if he thinks I think he killed his dad?" As the gardener passed behind the hedge again, the two women attempted to look nonchalant. Mother Grey ate much of her food and made small talk. *Snick snick* went the shears. At last his footsteps receded. Shannon peeked through the branches. He glanced around, almost as though he knew someone was spying on him, but she was almost sure he didn't see her this time. At last he disappeared through a small gate in the hedge into what appeared to be an enclosed part of the garden.

"Should we follow him?" Shannon asked.

"No. You could be right, he might be dangerous. I do think someone should speak to him about his father's death, but it ought to be the police. How does he know you?"

"He and his father were fighting, arguing, in Mr. Ferryman's kitchen when I was there."

"Indeed," said Mother Grey.

"I should have told the police about it. I wasn't thinking. But they would have thought I was making it up to save my father, don't you think? That's what Martine thought."

"The police should be told where he is, if only so they can notify him of his father's death. Wait for me here in the garden," Mother Grey said. "I'm going to try to find a phone."

Suddenly the clink of spoon on glass cut through the babble of conversation. When the crowd had fallen silent, a woman's voice said, "Two minutes, everyone. Mother and Dad are on their way. Get ready to shout 'Surprise.' "

Everyone tried to become unobtrusive, if not invisible. Shannon was squashed against the prickly hedge by a plump woman with a huge hat, an old-time garden party hat of ecru leghorn, covered with silk flowers. She had to bend her knees and hunker to see between the hat and the woman's shoulder. It took her a minute to figure out how to do this without getting stuck with hedge prickles.

"Tell me, Frida, why is this a surprise party?" said Hat Woman. "I would have thought surprises were dangerous at their age."

"They didn't want a party," her companion replied. "The last time my parents gave a party of any size, I was very small, but it was so ghastly that I still remember it. Something very unpleasant happened. My mother is so superstitious about parties even now that this one had to be a surprise."

"Or they wouldn't come?"

"Something like that."

"But then why—"

"Oh, come on, Mary, lighten up. It's their fiftieth anniversary, for God's sake."

"Ah. Here they come." The fat woman stood on tiptoe, shifting her hat upward, and Shannon was able at last to see the door they were watching, or a narrow sliver of it that showed behind the bench, under the armpit of the marble angel.

The crowd held its breath as the door swung slowly open.

12

It was deadly quiet in Jim Smith's study. Shannon would have been disappointed; the study was not the scholarly retreat of a thirties-movie wealthy gentleman but rather the decaying lair of an old, old man. A reclining lounge chair reeking of unwashed hair faced a large-screen television set. On one side of the chair was a stainless-steel walker with worn handgrips, on the other a telephone with big numbers; out of reach on top of the bookcase, a tray of pills. Between the lounge chair and the door to the adjacent powder room, a track in the carpet worn by shuffling feet.

The important-business desk that must have been here once was here no longer. The leather-covered books had gone unread for many a year. The eight-point buck whose head was mounted over the fireplace had been shot so long ago that had he escaped the bullets of the hunter, he and all his children would by now have died of old age. But the telephone worked. Picking up the receiver, Mother Grey heard a dial tone.

Shall I dial 911, she thought, *and spend half an hour establishing my credibility with the locals here, or shall I make a long distance call to the police in Fishersville, who know me?* No contest. It wouldn't cost the householders much more than a quarter, which they could clearly afford.

"I'll patch you through to Jack Kreevitch," said Rose, the clerk who answered the phone at the police station.

"You'll do what?"

"I mean, he's standing right here. Yo! Jack! It's Mother Vinnie."

She explained that John Ferryman's son could be found on the Jim Smith estate in Radderford, working as a gardener.

"We'll have the Radderford police send someone out to tell him his father's dead," Jack assured her. "Unless, of course, you want to tell him yourself, Mother Vinnie."

Of course, of course, it was her job to bring people bad news. But not this time. "It might be more complicated than that," said Mother Grey, thinking, *He might have killed the old man himself. Then what if he confesses? I'd have to make a citizen's arrest. He's a lot bigger than I am.* "I'd just as soon stay out of it for now," she said. "It would be better if the police talked to him."

"We'll send them, then," Kreevitch said. "You think that Mark Smith didn't do it, I take it."

"I'm not sure, Jack," she said. "I hope he didn't. His daughter is a nice person." A grandfather clock began to clang in the hallway, and when it finished striking seven, she thought of Dave Dogg. Right now he would be sitting by his telephone in the little house in Ewing Township that he shared with his ex-wife and their son. Should she call him from here? She thought of the Smiths' phone bill, a long list of strange calls appearing on it, perhaps leading to inquiries. People telephoning Dave next month, asking, what was this call? No. "I was supposed to call Dave at seven o'clock," she said to Jack Kreevitch.

"No kidding," he said. "You mean you two are, er . . . ?"

"No, I don't mean anything of the kind," she said. "But he's been trying to get in touch with me, and he's waiting by the phone. Would you just give him a call? Tell him I'm here," she said. "Tell him I'm just leaving. Tell him I promise I'll call him later, in about three-quarters of an hour, when I get home."

"Sure thing, Vinnie."

"I'm going as soon as I collect Shannon. Actually it would be good not to be here when the police arrive."

"You never minded before," Kreevitch said.

"It's nothing personal, Jack," she said. "I just don't want to do crime right now. And all of these people are strangers to me."

When she emerged from the dank unpleasant study into the hall, she saw that the party seemed to have moved indoors again. At the head of the table in the dining room, the elderly guests of honor had taken their places, a bald-headed old man in a wheelchair and his ancient wife with her hair dyed yellow and permed. Hovering over them was a slim, tense, smartly dressed woman who must have been their daughter, by her manner and the cast of her features. A huge cake sat before them, and piles of presents. Mother Grey's friend, the second-generation Hungarian caterer, popped champagne corks right and left and passed the bubbly around in crystal glasses.

"What should I do now?" the old man said.

"Make a toast, Dad," said the woman at his elbow.

"I don't know what to do."

"Raise your glass. Say, 'Here's to fifty more years.'"

"My glass?"

"Like this." She took his hand and lifted it, raising the glass for him, revealing a long white scar on his right forearm, reaching from the V formed by his thumb and forefinger nearly to the elbow.

The scar was like a bolt of lightning, forty years old. The wound from the broken window. This old man had to be James Waring Smith.

"To fifty more years," the daughter toasted, in a voice ringing with the false heartiness customarily used in speaking to small children.

"Fifty more years," said the old man, frowning, perhaps trying to figure out how long a period of time fifty years might be.

They all said, "Fifty more years," and everyone drank.

Children and grown grandchildren bustled around them, offering presents. The gifts appeared unimaginative to Mother Grey, if not mindless, more appropriate for a young couple starting their life together than two old people married fifty years. What in the world, for instance, would they want with another toaster? Suddenly the old woman directed her fierce hawklike gaze at the daughter, slammed her glass down on the table, and shouted, "This is not champagne!"

What was the story? Had they given her ginger ale? The daughter murmured to her, showed her the label on the bottle, and refilled her glass, whose contents had sloshed all over the table. Everyone else pretended not to notice.

The old man opened an envelope and took out some sort of travel tickets.

"Tickets for a cruise, Daddy," Frida said.

"What should we do with them?" he said.

"Get on a ship. Play shuffleboard."

"I don't know what to do. I think I should die."

What a merry party. James Waring Smith was going to be a lot of fun on that cruise ship. A real live wire.

"It will be fun," said the daughter. "You'll love it. There will be night club shows, wonderful food . . ."

The old woman leafed through a large, gold-stamped, leather-bound book entitled *Family History*. "Look, it's a picture of Mama. Is this from you, Kurt?" she said.

"No, that's from cousin Dieter. I gave you the marble angel," said a man who must have been the son. His face! *My word, it's Mark Smith.* Or someone with the family face, looking the way the old man did forty years ago, in the photographs in Mrs. Weeds's album. But this man's hair was longer, he was thinner, and he was much better dressed. "You must have seen the new angel. You passed it when you came into the garden. If you missed it, we can go back out and look." And his voice was nothing like Mark's. She remembered Mark Smith's speech as clipped and tentative, pitched more in the tenor range, where that of Kurt was a deep baritone, booming with confidence, colored with a Philadelphia accent.

What would Shannon make of all this? And where was she?

"Thank you, dear," the old woman said. "Thank you

very much. I love angels. You can show it to me later."
She drained her glass.

The daughter offered a toast of her own: "To my brother Kurt, bringer of angels, who has turned his life around so beautifully this past year."

"To Kurt," the old wife said, and everyone echoed, "Kurt."

"Should I drink?" the old man said.

The daughter continued: "Congratulations to Kurt on his new business enterprise, and best wishes for a wonderful life to him and to his new bride."

"Kurt," they all toasted again. The Mark Smith look-alike smiled and bowed.

"And a toast to his lady, my wonderful new sister-in-law, Felicia."

Again they all raised their glasses. "Felicia."

Felicia!

There she stood, Dave Dogg's ex-wife, Felicia.

During what Mother Grey thought of as Felicia's yo-yo period, when the unhappy woman kept bouncing back to Dave with her various personal crises—alcoholism, failed love affairs, painful resurgences of maternal instinct—the two women had contrived never to meet, which was easy enough since Mother Grey had herself broken up with Dave, yes, fifteen or sixteen times. But this was Felicia all right. Mother Grey remembered her hair particularly, a large wild mane, exactly like the large wild mane on this woman, and her startling dark eyebrows.

Married.

But of course Felicia was free to marry; although she had moved back in with Dave, they had never legally retied the knot.

Felicia! Married! And not to Dave this time!

"Kurt!" the old woman said. "You mean you're married to this girl? You got married again?"

"Yes, Mother."

"Why wasn't I there? Where was this wedding?"

"It was very quiet. A small civil ceremony. We thought—"

"Like your father and me." Old Mrs. Smith considered that for a moment, asking herself whether a small civil ceremony was acceptable, deciding it wasn't. "It's not like it's wartime. You should have had a wedding."

Felicia hugged his arm. The newlywed. "We're very much married, Mrs. Smith," she said.

Mrs. Smith squinted at Felicia, then back at her son. "Is she pregnant or what?"

Felicia was embarrassed. Everyone was embarrassed. Even Mother Grey would have been embarrassed, if her head hadn't been swimming with wonder at the spectacle of Felicia married. At last Kurt Smith filled the uncomfortable silence with a show of connubial lechery: "We just couldn't stay away from each other," he said. He took Felicia in his arms and kissed her. Not your usual party behavior, but what the heck, they hadn't been married very long. The assembled multitudes tittered, simpered, and cheered. Was she dreaming? Mother Grey gave her own arm a really hard pinch.

Over the new husband's shoulder, Felicia's gaze found Mother Grey's. Their eyes locked in a moment of startled recognition.

She came straight to her through the crowd, the Mark Smith look-alike trailing along behind her, and seized Mother Grey by her two arms. "Vinnie Grey?" she said.

"Yes, it's me. Hello, Felicia."

"This is wonderful!" she said, and embraced her. Mother Grey patted her back. Felicia felt like a bird, all tiny little bones. They stood back and regarded each other. "This is so wonderful. My husband—my ex-husband—is still in love with you, you know."

"Do tell," Mother Grey said. The thing about Felicia, Dave always said, was that she knew how to have fun. The other thing about her was that she did not know how to stop having fun. The breath on her was paralyzing. More than mere champagne, surely.

"But this is so fantastic. What are you doing here?" she said. "I want you to meet Kurt Smith. We were married this morning."

"We met at an AA meeting," Kurt Smith said cheerfully. Even close up he could have been Mark Smith's twin, except for the voice. Married this morning. Imagine that. *I don't care how much it hurts to pinch my arm. I know I'm dreaming this.*

Or could this have been what Dave wanted to tell her? I'm free at last, my needy ex-wife has dumped me for a rich guy from Bucks County?

"How do you do?" Mother Grey said, offering her hand. Kurt Smith released his grip on Felicia long enough to shake it.

"Kurt is in statuary," Felicia said, glowing, hugging him by the arm. The implication was, not a policeman. She had done better this time. "I came to Radderford to meet his family. Isn't it wonderful? His parents have been married for fifty years."

"Honey, are your bags all packed?" Kurt Smith murmured. "Our plane leaves at nine thirty-five. The cab will be here any minute."

"We're going to Saint Kitts," Felicia burbled. How happy she seemed to be, marrying money. *What does Dave think of all this? I have to talk to him.* Was Felicia pregnant? *Oh, for heaven's sake, who cares?*

"I want to wish you both every happiness," she said, casting wildly around for a way out. The old man's wheelchair was planted in front of the door to the front hall. "And you, Mr. Smith," she said to him. "Happy anniversary. Are you in statuary too?"

"Can you tell me where I'm supposed to go?" Jim Smith said.

"We retired several years ago, but sausage was our business," old Mrs. Smith said. "You've heard of Smith's Sausages."

"Of course," Mother Grey said. "I have them for breakfast all the time." Good too. You bought them in frozen links, and they fried up into the tastiest little sausages without a whole lot of trouble, tender yet crispy. . . .

Felicia, married to a rich Bucks County sculptor. This must be another of those dreams. And yet she felt as though some dark internal cloud had blown away, as though the radiant sun shone on her soul, which had become a thing of unimaginable lightness, rising into the blue sky. It was not, of course, the radiant sun of sanity. She understood this.

I know I'm dreaming.

Shannon Smith appeared in one of the front windows, strangely pale. Mother Grey had forgotten her! She must have been waiting out in the garden all this time; now it had begun to rain. Shannon's hair was streaming in her eyes. Why didn't she come inside?

"I must leave now," Mother Grey said, taking the old

man by the hand and maneuvering his chair away from the doorway. "It was a wonderful party. Have a very happy day." She squeezed his knobby knuckles. Outside, Shannon dodged behind a bush.

"You can wish him a whole month of happy days," the daughter said. "He's going on a cruise now. Isn't that exciting, Dad? By the way, I'm not sure I heard your name. I'm Frida Smith." She looked Mother Grey straight in the eye when she spoke these words, her gaze a bloodshot challenge, and lit a cigarette.

"Where am I going?" the old man said.

"Lavinia Grey," Mother Grey said. "A cruise! How nice. And is this a surprise?"

"Complete surprise. Mother tells me they never had a real honeymoon. Did you, Father?" As Frida picked a shred of tobacco off her lower lip, Mother Grey realized she was smoking a Pall Mall, unfiltered. One hardly saw those anymore. Her lipstick had come off on her teeth.

"No honeymoon," the old man agreed. "I don't know what to do now. I feel so sick. Wait. Don't go yet." He gripped her hand harder.

Frida blew a stream of smoke out of her nostrils. "Reverend Grey was just leaving, Dad," she said.

"Yes. I must go," she said, smiling. "Someone is expecting me."

A cold rain was sprinkling down on them as the two women climbed into the rental car and closed the doors.

"I saw him," Shannon said. Her teeth were chattering.

"I know," said Mother Grey. "It's him for certain. The

scar he got on the night of the flood is still on his arm. And the other son looks exactly like—"

"No, I mean I saw him the way Barton said. This is the place on the hill, a high place. He came in the garden gate, and there was the angel at his right hand. When people started taking pictures with their flashbulb cameras, he was surrounded by light. I knew it had to be him."

The child was in shock. "Wrap this blanket around yourself. What angel?"

"There's a marble angel in the back garden by the gate where Mr. Smith and his wife came in. One of the hands is missing. Mother Grey, I don't know whether I want to talk to him. After what he did to Nana—"

"An angel with a missing hand?"

"Yes. But suddenly there was—"

"Wait a minute. You saw that angel in Mount Outlook Cemetery by the graves of all those Rabsons. Could it be the same one?"

She pulled the blanket more tightly around herself. "I don't know. I never thought of that. But listen, that man from the cemetery is here, the one with the hair and the beautiful eyes. It's like my whole fate is here."

"Something is here," said Mother Grey, "and I think it's something pretty strange."

"Let's go."

"But listen. As long as we've come all this way to see your grandfather, don't you want to go and meet him before we leave? I have to warn you, he's very old, and his mind—"

"I have to get control of myself first," Shannon said. Her color was a little better. "I think I need a drink or something."

"You can get some champagne inside. It's flowing like water. I would see him, if I were you. Because he's leaving on a cruise in a little while, and he won't be back for a long time. Maybe not ever. He's very old and frail."

"Give me a minute to get myself together," Shannon said. "After that I'll go in."

"Okay," Mother Grey said. "And while you compose yourself, I'm going to check on something. Stay here. Don't leave the car."

"Where are you going?"

"I want to get a look at that angel you mentioned," she said. "It's probably nothing, but— It won't take a minute. Wait here." She took her handbag and the only umbrella.

13

There was a way after all to get into the back garden without going through the house. The caterer and his assistants came through a hidden gap in the hedge, carrying tables and trays to their truck. Mother Grey passed through the gap to find that it led to an unfamiliar part of the garden, not the lawn by the terrace, which she had already seen, but some part walled off from that. All alone with the hiss of falling rain and the smell of boxwood, Mother Grey began to wander the network of hedges and vine-covered stone walls.

A door in one of the walls gave onto a washyard. A washyard, in this day and age! Clotheslines were strung from pole to pole, but no clothes hung in the rain, nor were any of the servants in evidence. They must have spent a great deal of time hanging the sheets out to dry and taking them in again. This household was something out of another era. She backed out of the washyard and continued to wander the rat maze that was the grounds of the old Smith place. She came upon a carriage house, or was it a garage? She peeked through a window, and inside she saw a yellow rental truck and a black Mercedes-Benz.

Sounds of hammering and construction grew softer and louder as she moved now closer, now farther away from the housing development just to the west. The future, closing in.

Then, finally, she found it. At the edge of the garden was a sweet little trellis, painted white, all covered with vines. In the wall beyond the trellis was a small door or gate, and bending toward the gate in an attitude of benediction was a shining white marble angel on a pedestal, with a missing left hand.

The marble hand from Mount Outlook was still—where else?—in her handbag. She took it out and held it up to the angel's wrist for a perfect fit.

What did this mean?

First of all, since it was Kurt who had given his parents the angel, it meant that Felicia's new husband was involved somehow in the cemetery theft. Unless he had bought it from Ron Ferryman, not knowing it was hot. But Mother Grey had seen them together in Fishersville the morning of the graveyard robbery. When she was chasing after Ron Ferryman, trying to give him his camping equipment back, it was Kurt who drove the Mercedes-Benz that picked him up.

Shannon was right. Ron Ferryman had cleaned out Mount Outlook Cemetery, with whatever accomplices, and killed his own father when he caught him at it. After that they had brought the cemetery ornaments here to this house in the yellow truck she had seen. A killer, and he knew Shannon was here and that she recognized him.

She shouldn't have left the girl alone.

Through the mazelike grounds she rushed back to the car, making more haste the more she thought of what all this meant for her personally. Felicia's new husband was a crook. Maybe even a murderer. Felicia would be crushed. After he was arrested, Felicia would be . . . needier than ever.

How simple it would be to lie low and say nothing to the authorities until she was sure the happy couple were in the air and well on their way to Saint Kitts.

And how corrupt. A vicious murderer was walking free. The sooner he was apprehended, the better. *Never mind the impact this might have on my personal life. I must act swiftly, before I have time to meditate on how nicely things could work out for me if I didn't act at all.* With that thought in mind, Mother Grey bounded out of the hedge and sprinted across the lawn to the car.

But Shannon was gone.

Furthermore, so were many of the other cars. The dark green rental car now sat in lonely splendor in the middle of the lawn, a distinct embarrassment. Not having the key, Mother Grey couldn't even move it. Once again she went up the front steps and into the house.

Shannon was nowhere to be seen. The dining-room table with its pile of gifts was still the center of activity, though the crowd was thinning out and all the small children had left. A few guests lined up to take their leave of the old couple. Others, Smiths and Smith in-laws, were crowding around the presents, opening them, feeling them, admiring them. A gust of chill air and a spatter of rain came through the French windows. Someone had opened them to let out the smoke.

Among the relatives stood Shannon's heartthrob, the European film actor, he said he was, the one she considered to be part of her fate. He held the family history book, his anniversary gift, and was pointing out some feature of it to his aunt, old Mrs. Smith. Ah, family feeling. Ah, fate. Mother Grey glanced around for Felicia, who really was a part of her fate, one way or the other, quite apart from romantic flapdoodle. Felicia wasn't there either. Her new husband, Kurt Smith, stood all alone in the midst of the slowly departing throng, a point of stillness in the swirling, babbling party.

He was staring at his father and sipping on a glass of something brown. When she passed in front of his field of vision, he blinked and refocused on Mother Grey.

"You're a priest," he said.

"Yes."

"Episcopal."

"That's right."

"So is my younger sister. Are you also a lesbian nitwit?"

"Not that I'm aware of," Mother Grey said. *And you, are you a thief?* His breath was pungent with alcohol. Must have missed the last AA meeting. Or the last several.

"There's no God, you know," he pointed out. "You're wasting your time." His nose, unlike his brother's, was webbed with fine red lines.

"I think I'd like to meet your sister," she said. "She must be a woman of rare discernment, to stay away from your family gatherings."

He spoke very slowly and carefully. "A woman of

more discernment than you. What are you doing here, may I ask?"

Mother Grey glanced around the room and out into the garden. Was that Shannon out there? Dieter von Helden put the book down and slipped out through the French windows. "I'm here to wish your parents a happy anniversary," she said.

"Go ahead. If you can get through to them, you'll be doing well. My father, for example, is a walking corpse."

They could hear him whining, "Help me, please, I don't know what to do."

"I'm sorry you feel that way," Mother Grey said.

Kurt Smith took a swallow of his drink and began to philosophize. "The depressing part about this kind of dementia is the glimpse it affords us into the so-called human soul."

Whoopee. The merrymaking was nearly universal. Mother Grey hadn't had so much fun at a party since the time she dropped the punch bowl on her foot. "What do you mean?" she said.

"There's nothing there. It's all neurology."

She knew this wasn't true. But how to explain it? "Faith gives us the answer to that," she said.

"Right. But if you have no faith, there's no answer."

No answer and, for some, no reason to temper their own self-regard. She searched his face, so like his half-brother's, for marks of criminal activity. But then, it doesn't show, does it? Prison stamps itself on a man's features, but crime leaves no mark. Okay, the nose, but maybe that was alcohol or a bad sunburn on an Irish complexion.

"Tell me about the statuary business," she said. He looked at her for a long time without replying.

Suddenly Shannon appeared in the doorway to the terrace, gripping the tote bag in her two hands. She was wetter than ever, of course, since Mother Grey had taken the only umbrella in the car. But even beyond that her demeanor said, *I've just had an Experience.* At least she hadn't been killed. Now to get her away from here.

Shannon looked wildly around the room. Of all these strangers, nearly every one was related to her by blood or marriage. She was searching for her grandfather.

She stepped inside and brushed the wet hair from her face. When she saw Kurt Smith—her uncle!—she must have thought for an instant that he was Mark, for she blurted, "What are you doing here?"

Slowly he turned toward her; slowly his eyes focused on her wild face and streaming hair. "I know you," he said.

As soon as he spoke, she realized he wasn't her father. "You couldn't possibly know me."

"But I do. I've seen your face before, long ago. You came to my house and insulted my mother."

"No, I didn't," Shannon said.

He frowned. "No, of course you didn't. You're much too young. You weren't even born when that happened." He drained the contents of his glass.

A clacking of high heels on the stairs, and Felicia called out: "Darling, is the cab here yet?" She appeared in the archway, a carry-on bag in her hand. Her outer garment was a shawl embroidered with bright flowers; she was ready for the islands. "I thought someone said . . ." Something in Mother Grey's face, or something about the wet girl standing in the doorway, must have struck her with foreboding. Fear crossed her face. What did she know? What did she suspect?

How long would it take her to go running back to Dave?

Mother Grey shook Kurt Smith's hand, using both of her small hands, affecting heartiness. "Congratulations again on your marriage," she said. "I hope you'll both be very happy." *Or maybe you'll spend your wedding night in jail.*

What an idea. This was awful. She had to talk to Felicia. She dived into the hallway and led her archrival by her bird-bone elbow into the musty study. "Felicia, listen. Before you leave for the airport with this man, there's something you need to know."

Felicia pulled away. "I don't believe this. Who told you to meddle in my life? Go find Dave. Take him. He wants you. But leave me alone. I'm doing fine, Vinnie. There's nothing you can tell me about Kurt that I want to hear. Kurt is the best thing that ever happened to me."

"I know you don't want to hear it, but—"

From the other room came a horrible scream. The old lady was shrieking:

"Give me poison!"

14

If Felicia could not be persuaded that her future lay anywhere but with Kurt, so be it. Mother Grey abandoned her and went to see what had caused the screams of the elderly Mrs. Smith.

In the dining room the French windows framed a tableau of melodrama: the old lady stretching forth her bony finger toward Shannon; Shannon standing, arms akimbo, defiant in her wooden clogs; everyone else recoiling in attitudes of concern or horror. Except for the old man. Oblivious to the fuss, he sat with his back turned to them all, absently riffling through some envelopes among the presents.

The old lady began to shout again. "You! Here again! Give me poison, I want to die!"

Kurt Smith slipped past Mother Grey and murmured

something to a large man standing in the hall. Mother Grey assumed it was the butler; he had an old-family-retainer quality to him, even though he was young. As soon as Kurt Smith finished speaking to him, he sped away as though on some errand.

"Let's go, sweetheart," Kurt whispered to Felicia. "Smithers is bringing the car around. Wilson will get the rest of our bags."

The newlyweds slipped out the front door followed by Wilson—it must have been Wilson—with the bags. Through the rain-streaked window Mother Grey could see him putting the bags in the trunk as Felicia and Kurt Smith climbed into the front seat of the black Mercedes.

Wilson slammed the trunk lid shut. Smithers faded away in the direction of the garage. The golden porch light glistened on the wet black surface of the car. *Can you imagine? That car cost more than seventy thousand dollars.* A lot of . . . statuary.

"Aaaagh!" The old lady was at it again. She clutched her lace collar and fell back into her chair, her eyes rolling up into her head. Mother Grey wondered whether she was subject to fits. Something like this must have happened fairly often, for the hovering Frida was prepared. From the pockets of her well-tailored blazer, she produced an ampule, probably spirits of ammonia, and broke it under her fainting mother's nose.

The old lady sputtered and waved it away. "Ach! What are you doing to me?" A nurse appeared, uniformed all in white, and for a while both of them ministered to the old lady.

The taillights of the Mercedes disappeared down the driveway. How dark it was growing. Mother Grey pulled her mental socks up. Now to get the police after the honeymooning couple in time to keep them from getting on their plane.

Thereby sending Felicia straight back into Dave Dogg's arms.

But first to rescue Shannon. Daughter Frida had left her mother in the hands of the nurse and was attacking the girl. "Who are you?" she demanded. "Why are you here upsetting my mother?"

"Your mother remembers the night my grandmother came to this house," Shannon said. "They say I resemble her."

"Your grandmother?" Frida lit another pungent cigarette. "And who would that be, pray tell?"

"Mary Agnes Fitzroy Smith. She was married to your father."

Frida, squinting, hugging her elbows, staring at the girl, exhaled a long stream of smoke through her nose. "The night your grandmother— The last big party my parents ever gave was for Dad's thirty-second birthday. I was four years old. I remember that some woman came and broke it up. Was that your grandmother?"

"Yes," Shannon said. "Your father is my grandfather."

Frida's eyebrows went up. It was making sense to her at last. "And so you've come to claim your share of the sausage fortune."

"I know nothing about a sausage fortune. I came here to see my grandfather. All these years we were told he was dead."

"I have bad news for you, little girl. There isn't a whole lot left."

Shannon's white skin went suddenly red. "Keep it," she said. "That isn't what I came for. Keep it. Stick it up your—"

Mother Grey pulled her by the arm. "You're soaking wet," she said to Shannon. "Come on. We'd better go." The old lady, coming out of whatever it was she had been in, was calling for her daughter. Frida joined the circle of helpers, professional and otherwise, attempting to revive and cheer her. "Please," Mother Grey said.

But Shannon had unfinished business. "Not yet." Her face was still red, and white around the nostrils. "Not until I do what I came here to do."

She went up to her grandfather, where he sat considering the table full of presents, and put her face in front of his unfocused eyes.

"Grandfather," she said.

"What?"

"How could you do what you did to Mary Agnes?"

"Mary Agnes," he said.

"How could you do it to my father?"

"Mary Agnes. Take me away from here."

"They told him you were dead. He grew up fatherless."

"Could you open this?" he said, and handed her a wrapped present, possibly another toaster.

She put it aside. "Listen to me. You abandoned my father. Your son. Mark."

"I don't know what to do. Where should I go? Tell me where to go."

"You rotten old bastard." Long past time to get out of here. Mother Grey pulled urgently on Shannon's arm, but she shook her off. From the tote bag the girl took the bronze-colored shoebox and put it on the table in front of her grandfather.

"What's this?" he said, blinking. He picked it up in

his hands and tried to get the lid off. "I can't seem to open it."

"You'd better hope you can't open it, Grandfather. That box is full of the wrath of God. Mary Agnes is in there."

"Mary Agnes. Take me away from here. Take me home."

"You aren't right, are you? I came too late to make an impression. This is like some sort of bad dream." Again Mother Grey tugged her by the arm.

"I don't know what to do," the old man said. "Tell me what to do."

"John Ferryman was three times the man you ever were."

He turned the box over and over in his hands. "Will somebody open this?"

"John Ferryman spit on your gravestone every day."

"I have no gravestone. There's no future in it."

"Give me my grandmother back."

The old man shrugged. "Take her."

He put the box of ashes back on the table. Shannon reached over to take them. By then old Mrs. Smith had just about recovered. She sat up, looked around, and noticed Shannon about to remove a box from her collection of presents.

With surprising speed the old lady struggled to her feet and snatched the box. "Excuse me, I believe that's my property."

"No," said Shannon. "It's mine. Take your hands off it." They wrestled; the old lady's grip was remarkably strong. The other relatives plunged into the fray and defended Mrs. Smith, pushing and pulling at Shannon, all saying things like, "Who is she? What is she doing here? Who invited her?"

The girl stood back, panting. Mother Grey put an arm protectively around her shoulder. "I'm Shannon Smith. I'm Jim Smith's granddaughter. Give me my grandmother's ashes back."

"She's what?" said someone.

"First cousin once removed," someone else said.

"Let's make it twice, shall we? Wilson!" Frida called. The ever-helpful Wilson appeared. Close up, he looked even less like a stage butler. Something about his manner and the cast of his features suggested to Mother Grey that he had developed those muscles in the penitentiary weight room. "This woman is an impostor," Frida said to him. "Please show her the door."

"Yes, ma'am," he said, flashing a gold tooth. His voice was deep and resonant.

"And you with the collar," Frida said, rounding on Mother Grey. "Did my sister send you here?"

"Not exactly," said Mother Grey.

"Another impostor. Please go."

"We need that box first," said Mother Grey, thinking, *Impostor. My word, nobody ever called me that before.* "That box holds the ashes of my friend's grandmother. When you give it back to her, we'll be happy to go."

Old Mrs. Smith spoke up: "Call the police. Have them both arrested."

"Please call the police, by all means," said Mother Grey. Frida and Wilson exchanged a glance of wild speculation at these words. *Aha! I have them now,* thought Mother Grey. *Guilty, guilty, they're all in it together. But I'm starting to think like Mark Smith.* Wilson continued to propel Shannon firmly toward the front door.

"It's all right, Mother," said Frida. "I'll handle this." Suddenly she produced a firearm, whether from her clothes or from some nearby piece of furniture, Mother Grey was never sure. All she knew was that it was black, with a dull finish, and pointing straight at Mother Grey. "You'd better leave," Frida said. "The party's over."

Another of the help appeared. This must be Smithers, a twin to Wilson except for the earring, which he wore in the opposite ear.

"Won't you give us Mary Agnes's ashes first?" Shannon pleaded.

"Don't let them have this box," the old lady insisted. "There's clearly something very valuable inside." She was wrestling with the top, pulling.

Smithers raised his eyebrows at Mother Grey in a threatening fashion. "Good-bye," Frida said. "Give our best to dear Billy."

Billy. That would be Wilhelmine, the other sister, the priest. "I will if I ever see her," Mother Grey said. So there was nothing for it but to leave. Wilson and Smithers showed them to the rental car. Then they stood on the lawn with their arms crossed over their muscular chests watching Shannon and Mother Grey drive out between the stone lions.

"We have to get to a phone," Mother Grey said. "I found the angel."

Still upset, Shannon seemed scarcely to understand what she had said. "What?"

"These people looted the cemetery in Fishersville."

"What people?"

"Ron Ferryman, almost for certain, and probably some if not all of the Smiths."

Shannon pulled the car over onto the shoulder. "Are you sure?"

Mother Grey opened her bag and showed Shannon the hand. "This is the hand you found in Mount Outlook Cemetery after the statues were stolen. It fits on the broken wrist of the angel in the garden here."

They were still within sight of the stone lions of the Smith establishment, but Wilson and Smithers were no longer standing on the lawn watching them. "Get going," Mother Grey urged. "If I don't call the police in the next five minutes, I'll lose the will to do it."

"Why would you do that?"

"Remember the man on my answering machine? Your uncle Kurt's new bride is his ex-wife. Now that she's safely on her way to Saint Kitts, he's mine. And you're perfectly right; I am in love with him. To live without true love may not be impossible, but it's disagreeable."

"Take him, then," Shannon said. "I'm happy for you. Be happy for me; he's here."

"Who?"

"The great love of my life. The man in the cemetery. I told you."

"The man in the cemetery?"

"Dieter von Helden."

"What makes you think Dieter von Helden is the great love of your life? You just met him yesterday."

"I don't know. Because he has yellow hairs on his arms. Because his kiss is paralyzing."

"He was kissing you?" *Now I feel really stupid,* thought Mother Grey, *going on that way about Dave; it's probably the same sort of thing.* The great love of her life.

She met him yesterday. He gives nice kisses. They don't even speak the same first language.

"He's a movie actor. Did you know that? In his own country. His career is just about to take off. He knows this director who's going to let him invest in her film and give him the starring part."

"Invest what?"

"What do you mean?"

Maybe he helped to loot the cemetery. But you can't say a thing like that to a woman in love. "I think you'd better put that romance on hold and get out of here. If I don't call the police soon, we'll be no better than accessories."

"But if you do call them, you'll lose your man."

"I will?"

"Isn't that what you just told me?"

"Never mind that now," said Mother Grey. *Get thee behind me, Satan.* So Shannon started the car. But a hundred yards beyond the end of J. W. Smith's vine-covered stone wall, she turned into the entrance road for the Radderford Woods development.

"I'm not leaving Nana's remains with those barracudas," Shannon said. "Besides, I have to say good-bye to Dieter."

15

Mother Grey's entire stock of subtle woodcraft came into play as she and Shannon approached the looming bulk of the house of Smith, where the ashes of Nana reposed in a bronze-colored box amongst the anniversary presents. Fortunately the Smiths had no dogs, or at least none that she knew of. Nevertheless it was too dark to creep around in the bushes. Mud was getting all over her good gray suit.

"Whatever possessed you to take those ashes out of the tote bag?" Mother Grey whispered.

"I can't tell you. It was something mystical, a gesture of power."

"And having done that, why did you let that woman take them away?"

"I don't know that either. It all happened so fast."

They crouched lower in the azaleas. By the light that streamed though the French windows, Mother Grey could see tiny cracks of magenta in the swelling azalea buds. Only ten feet of flagstone terrace lay between them and the windows, still open a crack to ventilate the dining room, overheated with partying. Mary Agnes's box of ashes was clearly visible on the dining-room table.

There was no one in sight, either within the house or without. Voices came from somewhere nearby. Behind the hedge they could hear a squirrel chattering, *kk-kk-kk*. A songbird called overhead. Would anyone notice if they slipped inside and took the ashes? "We could make a diversion," Mother Grey suggested.

"There's a diversion already," Shannon whispered. "Everyone's out front getting into the limousine or saying good-bye."

It was true. Beyond the table, covered with presents, through the gleaming front hall, and beyond the open door, they could just see Wilson and Smithers wrestling a steamer trunk out and down the steps.

"Stay here," said Mother Grey. "If I get caught, go for the police." She rose from the bushes and strolled casually across the terrace.

No one saw her widen the crack in the door, or noticed the small squeak it made when it opened; no one saw her slip inside and go straight to the gift-laden table. She nearly had the ashes in her possession, but Dieter's *Family History* was irresistible. She flipped it open and saw that the Smiths traced their ancestry clear back to County Cork. *We could be cousins,* she thought, flipping to the earliest part of the history. The brown leather binding felt smooth and warm, the soft warmth of real calfskin. Old pictures appeared here and there, scanned in before the pages were printed on a good color laser printer. Prim women in black dresses, mustachioed men in high collars.

The leather cover smelled good too. A nice job. Not surprisingly, she found that Mary Agnes's line was nowhere represented.

Voices and sounds floated in the open front door: "Where should I go? I don't know what to do." The car door slammed. The engine started. Tires crunched on gravel, rolling away. She heard more voices approaching. Rats. Too late to get away. She dropped behind the table and slid under the snowy damask cloth and found that the rug was covered with crumbs. Well, that's what happens when you don't have a dog.

Wilson came in, talking. "Clean up in here and lock the doors," he said. "The Smiths won't be back till the twentieth of May, Miss Frida said, so I'll be wanting you back here on the nineteenth to dust and get everything ready."

"I cover the furniture now?" said a woman's voice, accented, perhaps Hispanic.

"I don't know if you have to do that," Wilson said.

"Be easier later if I cover the furniture now."

"All right, then. There's some muslin in the upstairs linen closet."

"What about these things?"

"I'll take anything valuable and put it in the safe, and whatever is left you can just— What the—?"

"Something wrong in that box?"

"Ashes. Nothing in it but ashes."

"Not valuable."

"Yeah, not valuable."

"I go get the muslin."

"Good. Don't forget to vacuum the furniture before you cover it."

"Okay."

Both sets of feet left the room through different doorways. Mother Grey got to her own feet, cramped from crouching under the table. The box of ashes was ready to hand. After checking to be sure it was securely closed, she slipped it into her bag. The French windows were still unlocked.

Shannon was not in the azalea bushes where Mother Grey had left her, but this had ceased to be surprising. No doubt she was wandering the grounds chasing after the Great Love of her Life. Ah, youth! No denying that the man was very handsome. Mother Grey could go for him herself if she went for mysterious, handsome foreigners, instead of ordinary, familiar, comfortable men like Dave Dogg, who was cute in his way but not breathtakingly handsome. In fact, he still resembled a fireplug, all the more so now that his red hair was thinning.

The hammering and banging in the housing project one field over had long since fallen silent and could not be used as a navigational aid. Wandering the rat maze of the grounds in the darkness, Mother Grey found that she had lost all sense of direction again. From time to time she called out in a stage whisper: "Shannon!" But there was no answer.

There was a faint glow that she thought came from the house. *I'll work my way back there and start over*, she thought. But after yet another wrong turn, the garage appeared before her.

The yellow truck that used to be inside was now parked out on the pavement in front, partway under a bright light mounted over the garage door. Arguing voices sounded. She ducked down behind the bushes but could not bring herself to run away; she wanted to eavesdrop. On the other side of the truck she saw two pairs of feet.

I am fated to look at people's feet today. What would Claudine say to that? *Feet are your fate, Mother Grey, I feel it.* Stop thinking silly thoughts and listen.

The argument was a business discussion, and the arguers were Dieter von Helden—or another fellow with a Viennese accent—and some local.

"I can't wait a month for my share of the profits," the local said. "I need money now."

"As you know, I have to dispose of the merchandise before I can realize any profits to distribute," von Helden said.

"And while we're on the subject, what do you mean letting your cousin give that angel away? It was the most valuable piece in the cemetery."

"It's not your business," said von Helden.

"I think it is. We were going to split this three ways."

"We didn't split the risks three ways, though, did we? I was the one who had to take care of that old man."

"Who asked you to?"

"He knew you. He would have turned you in."

"Of course he knew me. He was my father. If anybody greased the old bastard, it should have been me. Why should I pay you to do it?"

"Let it go, Ronnie."

"He saw you. That's why you hit him. Here you're getting all set to be a famous movie star. You thought he would know your face when you got famous. Turn *you* in. Right?"

"I told you. Forget about it."

"So don't talk to me about risk. Everybody is at risk. Talk to me about money."

"Yes?"

"I want five grand to last me till you come back with the rest. That's now, before you get on the fuckin' boat."

"What you ask is impossible. Let it go."

"Suppose I don't choose to. Three-way split was the agreement. I want what's coming to me, and two grand up front."

"Okay, asshole," the German said. He said, "Ah-sole," not the way the word was pronounced in New Jersey. Then came the sound of another squirrel, or maybe someone having a bad asthma attack, *ukk-ukk-ukk.* "Take what's coming to you. Two-thirds–one-third is a better split anyway."

A sack of heavy rags dropped to the asphalt next to the truck; Mother Grey could see it; but no, it was . . .

"Dieter!" cried Shannon, jumping out of the bushes. "I couldn't leave without saying good-bye. What's that? Oh, my God."

What followed was deeply embarrassing when Mother Grey thought about it later. When Shannon saw the strangled, dead body of Ron Ferryman and Dieter (the Great Love of her Life) standing over it with a ligature in his hands. she did that thing that birds are said to do when they look into the eyes of a snake. She just stood there. No screaming, no running, just standing. Mother Grey could see her feet.

Of course Mother Grey should have sneaked away at that point and gone for the police. But what could she do? Her blood was up. And there was Shannon, in peril of her life.

And then Dieter grabbed her. Or at least Mother Grey assumed he grabbed her, from the scuffling and muffled shrieks.

So Mother Grey attacked him.

Then there ensued the most profoundly humiliating God-awful struggle, in which the two women, weaponless except for Shannon's car keys, greatly overmatched in size and strength, attempted to get the better of Ron Ferryman's murderer, with the victim's still-warm body tangled under their feet. There was bellowing, snarling, cursing, eye-gouging, ball-kicking, biting, and pure ugliness on everyone's part.

The shame of it was that they did all that for nothing. Wilson came running when he heard the noise and evened up the fight. Mother Grey found that she had behaved in that disgraceful way to no ultimate effect.

I should have run away, she berated herself, silently perforce, since the gag in her mouth kept her from complaining out loud. And sometimes, *I should have bitten him harder.*

She couldn't remember the last time she had heard such a bad person uttering so much oily self-serving chat. The whole time he was tying them up, he ran off at the mouth, partly for their benefit and partly to quiet the bad conscience of Wilson, who might have been some sort of felon but not a murderer.

Von Helden paused for breath, and Wilson said, "I don't waste women."

"Waste not, want not," Mother Grey mumbled. She must have been punch-drunk to speak up at all, still less to say something silly, instead of using her legendary powers of persuasion to get Wilson to let them go. Dieter von Helden whacked her smartly on the side of the head and stuffed a gag in her mouth.

After that she had plenty of time to get a good close look at the kitchen linoleum. It was amazing how a seemingly solid piece of linoleum could be so full of tiny little cracks.

"I don't like to kill people either. Not at all," Dieter said. "I'm not one of these guys who likes to go around killing people."

"What about him?" said Wilson, gesturing toward something behind Mother Grey's back.

"I promise you, it was just business. He expressed some unreasonable objections to our arrangements."

Wilson just rolled his eyes. She saw his hands holding a pocketknife, frightening until he used it to sever the dangling end of the rope he had tied her up with and then put it away.

"Then what about John Ferryman?" Shannon said.

"Who?" Dieter said.

"Ron's father. The old man in the graveyard. He killed another man, you know," she said to Wilson. "You'd better look out for him."

"Did that old man die? I'm sorry. I was only trying to shut him up. Business again. You see, it would ruin my business if I had to go to jail." He popped the gag in her mouth and, grunting, tightened her bonds. "I'm sure you wouldn't like it—mh—either—mh—Mr. Wilson. An unpleasant place. There."

"I hear you," said Wilson. "Never liked it before. Okay, let's get out of here."

"One more thing we need to do," von Helden said. He turned a handle and unlatched a big solid door in the kitchen wall, which swung slowly open, letting out a blast of icy air.

"You ain't gonna put them in there. They'll be dead in a half hour."

"Don't worry about it. We'll make an anonymous call to the police. They'll come in no time at all and let them out. Come on, now. Heave."

The two men dragged Ron Ferryman's remains through the door. Movie fog was rolling out of the freezer. Mother Grey perceived that the door was lined all around with a rubber gasket, and she thought, *This is going to be unpleasant.* She watched them working in the foggy shadows, hoisting Ferryman's body onto a meat hook.

At his hip the blades of the hedge clippers gleamed. He wasn't much, Ron Ferryman, but at least he kept his tools clean. Or maybe he hadn't worked here that long. Hedge clippers. If she could get them, perhaps she could cut their bonds. The thought had scarcely formed in her mind when von Helden noticed the direction of her gaze.

"Ah!" he said. "This could be an unfortunate oversight." He unbuckled the leather tool carrier from around the waist of the dead man. "We wouldn't want you tinkering with my plans, now, would we?" He flung it into a corner of the kitchen and, together with Wilson, proceeded to drag the women one by one into the freezer and secure them to opposite sides of a circular shelf that occupied the middle of the space, keeping up a constant stream of chatter the whole time.

And a small space it was. Already Mother Grey was feeling uneasy, and that was with the door open.

"Well, ladies, I could stay here all night and talk philosophy with you, but we have a boat to catch. *Auf*

Wiedersehen. Or should I say, good-bye. I don't expect us ever to meet again, not in this life, and probably not in the next either."

Shannon made some sort of sound, which must have touched his feelings somehow, for he felt compelled to say, "I promise you, you two ladies are perfectly safe. Just remain quiet for ten more minutes, and I'll send someone to let you go."

Of course he was lying; either he meant to wait until Wilson had left, go get the cord he had used on Ron Ferryman, and strangle them here before they thought of a way to get away, or he meant to leave them to die in the freezer, trussed up like these other cuts of meat.

"I promise you," he said again, and closed the freezer door. Well built, well sealed, it made a very solid thump. Air pressed against Mother Grey's eardrums.

Through the small glass window embedded with chicken wire, a beam of dirty light came in, barely enough for her to see her breath as it puffed out of her nose and turned to frost. The cords were tied too tight for her to get her hands loose, wriggle though she might, but she hitched around toward Shannon, who hitched around toward her, until they were close enough to keep each other warm.

It seemed as though a lot of time went by. Mother Grey chewed through her gag. Then she used her teeth to untie the knot in Shannon's gag. As soon as the gags were off, the two of them yelled and screamed at the tops of their voices. No one came.

Shannon began to sob with frustration and terror. This wouldn't do. If they lost their heads, they would never get out. "Don't cry," she said. "This sort of thing happens to all my sidekicks. We always get out of it."

Shannon sniffled and wiped her nose on her shoulder. "What makes you think I'm the sidekick? Maybe you're the sidekick."

Lavinia Grey, the sidekick. Not the center of the universe, perhaps not even the center of what was going on. "You're right, of course." Trust the young to keep you humble.

"Move your hands closer, Mother Grey. I have two fingers loose. Maybe I can—" They struggled with their bonds in silence for a while, until Mother Grey began to brood over the nature of Dieter von Helden.

"So," Mother Grey said, "the great love of your life."

"Hey, anybody can make a mistake."

Mother Grey tore a fingernail on the rope, down past the quick. As she worked on the knots, it began to throb. "I wish I had bitten that man a lot harder."

"I wish I had taken his eye out," Shannon said. "Do you know you can use a set of keys to permanently disable somebody? They taught me that in a self-defense course I took once. There, that knot is undone."

The knot in question had been restraining Mother Grey's right hand. Freedom! What a relief! It was the work of a moment to free her left hand too. She rubbed her two hands together. Now for Shannon's ropes, and the ropes on her own ankles, and after that phase two, where they broke out of the freezer. Phase three would be where they got in the car and drove as far from Radderford— "Was that the car key you were trying to use on his eye?"

"The key to the rental car, yes."

"I hope you still have it." Maybe they wouldn't be driving home after all. Maybe they would have to hitchhike.

"It might have dropped on the ground in the scuffle. I'll search my pockets as soon as you free my hands. I know it isn't in my bag. I left that in the car."

"The bag with the shovel in it?"

"Right."

"Too bad." Mother Grey had been entertaining fantasies of tunneling out of the freezer. "I don't know where my bag is." But that was the least of her worries.

They finished untying each other.

Shannon couldn't find the car keys anywhere. It was dark, and as she groped, she complained of losing feeling in her fingers. "We could light a fire, if we had matches. Do you think he smoked?" She indicated the corpse with a toss of her head.

"I think I remember seeing him with a cigarette," said Mother Grey, weighing whether it would be worthwhile to search the body, and whether it would be possible to manage it without seeing his face again.

"So maybe he has matches." A long moment while they eyed his pockets, then each other to see who would be first to touch him. Then simultaneously the two women put their shuddering reluctant hands in Ron Ferryman's pockets and felt around. Mother Grey came upon the matches together with half a pack of Marlboros, while Shannon retrieved what appeared to be a set of car keys. "Hey," she said, "these are mine."

"Are you sure?"

"No, they're different. But the rental company is the same."

"See if there's something to burn," said Mother Grey. "Fire, meat—we could live in here very comfortably until somebody finds us." She stretched her cramped arms, and suddenly experienced a sensation of light-headedness such as she hadn't known since the time she and Stephen went climbing in the Canadian Rockies and tried to do too much too soon. Cold, it was that time, or altitude, or . . .

Lack of oxygen.

"On second thought, no fires," she said.

"Why?"

"Oxygen. We're running out of air."

16

The last servant had left for the allotted month's vacation. To the east of the Smiths' acreage, a full moon appeared between luminous streaks of cloud cover, bringing the skeletons of roofless new houses into sharp relief. Highway traffic had thinned to an occasional automobile, passing the stone lions with a whoosh. A distant bird warbled its last song of evening.

Dieter von Helden glanced around the yard, checking to be sure he had left nothing visibly out of order. If its appearance remained untroubled, the house might not be disturbed for as long as it took for his plans to bear fruit. In another month the cargo of statues would be profitably disposed of to the buyer in Marseilles, the elder Smiths would be installed in the nursing home, and the younger ones would be in a position to deal discreetly with the bodies in the freezer. In two months Liesl's motion picture would be well into production. In six, Dieter von Helden would be a household name.

But there must be no outward clues visible from the public areas to attract the attention of the law.

Between the haunches of the crouching lions shone the headlights of a car, illuminating for an instant the roots of the hedge and a handbag lying where the woman priest had dropped it.

Von Helden froze. Had the driver seen it? For the car rolling up the driveway was a police car. Why was he coming here? That sentimental idiot Wilson must have called the police before he left and told them to come and release the two women.

There was no way von Helden could avoid the attention of the person in the car; he was standing in plain sight on the front porch. The policeman waved languidly as the car rolled to a stop in front of the house.

Why did I take so long to pack up? Von Helden cursed himself. Two minutes later, and he and the truck would have been far away. He could still be safe, though: those women in the airtight freezer were dead by now, surely; they couldn't identify him. His best chance was to persuade this policeman he had just arrived.

The officer got out of the car. He was dressed in plain clothes, a windbreaker and slacks, but he carried himself with a certain authority, and his eyes flickered around in the way policemen everywhere have of examining their surroundings for the unusual. The handbag lay in shadow under the hedge. The man would have had to be a cat to see it. He called out to von Helden: "Good evening, sir."

Von Helden rehearsed a few stories in his mind. *First*

of all, it's important to make him think I just arrived.
"Good evening," he said. "Is there something I can do for you? I just got here." Bad. He should have said something smoother. *I just got here, by the way. By the way, I just got here, I promise you.*

"I'm looking for a Mr. Ronald Ferryman," the policeman said. "Would you happen to know where I could find him?"

"Ronald Ferryman?" A horrific image formed in von Helden's mind of Ferryman, face purple, tongue protruding, dangling from a meat hook in the freezer. "Why, no," he said. The image turned slowly from side to side.

"Is something wrong?" the policeman said.

"I couldn't say. I just got here. Just arrived."

"This is the home of James W. Smith, isn't it?"

"Oh, yes. Yes." The policeman appeared to expect something more, so von Helden said, "My uncle."

"I wasn't sure," the policeman said. "There isn't any number on the front." He glanced at the neighboring houses across the hedge, although they were clearly uninhabited, some not even finished. Did he think James Smith might live over there? Von Helden felt a surge of confidence. This man was stupid. Also he was short. *I can take him easily.*

"Well, then, can you tell me whether your uncle employs a man named Ronald Ferryman?" the policeman asked. "He would be working as a gardener."

"He might. I can't be sure. The staff is very large here. I myself am visiting."

The policeman gave him a sharp look, and for an instant von Helden expected him to ask him for his papers, but he said, "Perhaps I could speak with someone more familiar with the household."

"The servants have been given a long holiday. Mr. Smith is on a cruise. I was just leaving."

The policeman's look became sharper. "I thought you just got here."

"I just got back here from an errand, and now I must collect my bags and return to Vienna. Is there some problem?"

"I'm afraid I have some bad news for Mr. Ferryman."

"What is it? I'll tell it to him."

"I think I'd better deliver this news myself. Do you mind if I look around for him?"

"As I explained, the servants have all been given the month off. I'm sure he isn't here."

Their eyes locked. It was one of those trials of will, where the superior man triumphs.

Sure enough, von Helden prevailed; the policeman dropped his gaze and put his tongue in his cheek, which gave his face an expression of stupidity. Stupid, stupid. Next von Helden would talk him into leaving. Within minutes the police cruiser would be rolling away into the sunset, and von Helden would be getting into the rented truck and heading for the docks of Port Elizabeth with his load of bronze and statuary, there to rendezvous with the cargo ship. At first light he would be bound for Marseilles, where the buyers would give him more than enough money for Liesl's film. And the partners, of course. Partner. Kurt Smith would expect his cut.

"Just the same," the policeman said, "I don't know how I could go back and have to tell them I came all the way here and never even tried to find this person."

"You say he's a gardener?"

"That's what they told me."

"Good. Let's look around the grounds, then." He led

the fellow down the steps again and around the front of the house, as far as possible from the boxwood hedge in whose deep shadow lay the black leather bag of the doomed priest.

"Mr. Ferryman," they called, first the policeman and then von Helden. It was growing very dark. Receiving no answer, finding no gardener, they came to the gate in the wall that led to the grounds in back.

"More gardens back there?" the policeman said. "That's probably where he is, don't you think? A gardener?"

"I wouldn't know," said von Helden, "but we can always look, can't we?" He stepped back and invited the officer to go first, but the man waited stolidly for him to lead the way, and for an instant von Helden thought he suspected him of something. A glance at his blank, bovine expression reassured him. So von Helden passed through the gate and led the officer up the garden path.

They proceeded to explore the maze of walls and hedges. The policeman carried a large flashlight, and he aimed its beam everywhere, but especially downward, in places where one might look for a crouching person hiding, or a body. All the while von Helden kept telling him that the servants had gone away.

"I'm sure this Ferryman person, whoever he is, isn't here either," von Helden said.

"Begins to look that way. Could you tell me where his living quarters are?" Over the top of the next hedge, the garage roof loomed against the sky, so von Helden told him about the servants' rooms over the garage. Wilson and Smithers lived there. Showing their quarters to this cop should be safe enough, if Wilson hadn't left anything incriminating lying around.

The beds were unmade, but as soon as the policeman had satisfied himself that no one was hiding in the rumpled covers, or under the beds themselves, or in the closets, he seemed ready to abandon his quest.

Until he came out the door and stood in front of the garage. Suddenly the motion-detecting light flicked on and illuminated the cab of the rental truck standing in the driveway.

The policeman walked around behind the truck. "What's in here?"

"Surely you don't think Mr. Ferryman is in the back of this truck."

"If he's in the truck," said the policeman, "I'm sure he'll speak up." He banged on the back door of the rental truck with the flashlight. "Hello in there!"

"No answer, as you see, Officer," von Helden said. "He can't possibly be in the truck."

"Just the same I'd like a look inside." The flashlight illuminated the large padlock that secured the back doors.

If this man saw the stolen goods, he might not realize they were stolen. After all, stolen goods were not what he had come to find. (What had he come to find? A servant to tell bad news to? He seemed curiously persistent for a person on such a trivial errand.)

Even so it was a risk. As soon as he suspected the truth, out would come the gun and the handcuffs, and Dieter von Helden would be off to one of those grossly unpleasant American prisons Wilson had told him about, full of large felons offering unwanted intimacies. "Wait a minute," von Helden said. "I'll pull the truck under the light for you."

He had thought of another option. He could crush

this policeman under the wheels of the truck, hide the body, and make a dash for Port Elizabeth.

He fitted the key into the ignition.

It was the wrong key.

He got out of the cab again. The policeman was looking at him with a very acute blue gaze. Worse, he was holding that priest's black handbag.

"Ah!" von Helden said. "You found it! How lucky."

"This?"

"Yes. My cousin Wilhelmine Smith's handbag. She's a priest, you know. They have to carry very plain handbags, it's part of the . . . If you'll just let me have that, I'll see that she—"

"You say this belongs to your cousin?"

"Yes. The Smiths are her parents, you see. Mr. and Mrs. Smith. They live here." The policeman put his hand in the bag and drew out a small morocco-bound Book of Common Prayer. "Her prayer book. As I said, my cousin is a priest of the Episcopal Church."

"How about that," said the policeman. He put the book back in the bag, apparently without noticing the initials *L.G.* stamped in gold on the cover. "Here you go." To von Helden's immense relief, he gave him the handbag, but then he said, "I hope you know where to find a key to this truck, sir, because I would really like to see what's inside it."

"Inside the truck."

"Yes. Now. If you don't mind."

Von Helden thought of demanding to see a warrant, but no, his best chance was to continue to lull this man's suspicions until he could get under his guard and kill him. "Ah, that's the problem, isn't it. I don't have the right keys with me. I would be happy to open the truck for you, but I don't seem to have the key." For he was definitely going to have to kill him. It was too bad; the man would be missed. Much easier to keep attention away from the house if there were no hue and cry. But the alternative—prison—was unthinkable.

"Hope you don't mind," the policeman said, and with a few sharp strokes he hammered the lock off the back of the truck with the flashlight. Then he turned the door handle and swung open the doors. "Hello in there," he called.

Inside the truck the stolen benches and statues, swathed in quilted padding, had an evil look, like stiff dead bodies. Would those women be stiff when this guy found them? Von Helden imagined him opening the freezer door, the women's faces staring, dead, blue, blue as that of the strangled Ronald Ferryman.

"What is this?" the policeman said.

"Statues. Benches. My cousin is in statuary."

"I wonder if you'd mind showing me the statuary."

"No problem," von Helden said. He climbed up into the truck. One by one he unwrapped the statues and benches, shifting them as necessary, while the policeman satisfied himself as to what each one was. Long after any other law enforcement officer would have recognized a cargo of contraband cemetery ornaments, the policeman kept von Helden at his task of unwrapping and displaying, unwrapping and displaying, until the very last bundle was identified. Von Helden asked himself: Why did he want to see every one? It must be that he had no interest in the statues, railings, and bronze doors as such, no matter where they came from. It must be that he was looking for Ronald Ferryman.

And expecting to find him dead.

198

While he shifted and wrapped the statues and benches, von Helden considered his next move. What was the problem with the keys to the truck? Ah, yes, Ron Ferryman had them. These would be the keys to that woman's car; she must have dropped them in the struggle. No doubt the real truck keys were still on Ferryman's body.

He would have to go back to the freezer, then, just as soon as he dealt with this cop. After that the cop could join the other dead meat.

A plan, a plan. First of all, get him in the house. In the kitchen were many sharp knives. Better yet, a gun. Cousin Frida owned one. Distract the policeman's attention, get him off guard, and shoot him in the back. Almost certainly the gun would still be in the house; the Smiths were flying to Florida to board the cruise ship, and guns could not be taken onto airplanes.

Where do American women keep their guns? In a drawer by the side of the bed. Or no, she had been waving it around in the dining room earlier. Perhaps in the drawer of the sideboard, along with the silver.

So it was necessary to first get him inside. Von Helden put back the last piece of statuary and closed the door to the truck, trying to think of some ruse.

The policeman said, "If you happen to have a key to the house, I would really like to see the inside." The ruse was unnecessary, after all.

Stupid policeman, lamb to the slaughter. Nothing more was required than to find the gun and get behind him. Von Helden concealed his smile. "A simple matter," he said. "They keep a key over the lintel."

* * *

The air in the freezer was growing so thin and cold that it was all Mother Grey and Shannon could do to stay alert. Shannon, at least, had shucked out of her wet clothing and put on, with loathing and shuddering, the dry coveralls of the hanging corpse. Good thing it was too dark to see him hanging there in his underwear.

Shannon didn't think much of Mother Grey's escape plan.

"This is your plan?" Shannon said. "To take two sides of beef down off these hooks and cover them with burlap? I don't see the point. I'm not even sure we're strong enough to do it."

"You work with what you have," said Mother Grey.

"Okay. What do we have?"

"A freezer full of meat, a pile of burlap rags, and Ron Ferryman's dead body with everything he had on him, including the key to the rental truck with the cemetery loot."

"Which Dieter has to come back for, if he wants to drive the loot anywhere."

"Right," said Mother Grey. "All we have to do is prepare him a proper reception."

"By fixing up dummies of ourselves."

"Yes. He comes back for the keys. He doesn't expect us to be hiding, waiting to run out and shut the door as soon as he's occupied with searching Ferryman's body for the keys."

"He won't notice that Ferryman's pockets are gone?"

"You think of something, then." Mother Grey was getting cross. "But hurry up. I'm going to pass out in a minute."

"Okay. I'm sorry. Tell me again."

"He comes in. He thinks we're lying under the burlap. It's too dark in here to see anything. He comes in a little farther. We run out and shut the door."

"It might work," Shannon said.

"Sure it will." *If he comes back soon enough.* Mother Grey leaned against the wall. The smallest effort was growing more and more difficult.

"Okay, I can see it," Shannon said. "He comes into the freezer."

"Right."

"He sees the two women hiding under the burlap. He whips out his trusty six-shooter and goes blam, blam, blam, blam, blam, blam into their quivering, still-warm bodies, only to discover that he has pumped his last bullets into two sides of beef."

"Don't make me laugh. It uses oxygen. Anyway, who says we're still warm?"

"Well, we're quivering," Shannon said.

"Shivering is more like it."

"Sh. I hear something. He's coming." Shannon put out her hand as though to steady herself. On the shelf she touched a wrapped package in the shape of a club. "Ah!" she said. "A leg of lamb." She picked it up and stood next to the door, holding it over her shoulder, waiting for the pitch. Mother Grey crouched behind her.

The noise grew louder and more well defined. It was coming not from the kitchen outside but from the back wall of the freezer, where the coils were. It was the refrigeration machinery making that sound. He wasn't coming.

As it continued to rattle and clank, Mother Grey had to face it: They would be unconscious by the time von Helden returned, or dead, by freezing or suffocation.

"Give me that," she said. Taking a good backswing

with the leg of lamb, she struck the small frosty window with all the strength she had left. The impact of the blow jarred the bones in her shoulders.

Von Helden quickly perceived, once inside the house, that the policeman wanted to go and look in directions opposite to wherever he wanted to lead him. The trick was to make him think he didn't want to go into the dining room, or that he didn't care. The trick was to appear unconcerned, allowing his adversary to wander into the dining room of his own accord.

It wasn't difficult. Von Helden viewed it as an acting exercise. He reviewed his motivation, the mild and helpful interest of an innocent bystander. He tried a sense-memory of a leisurely warm bath. He banished from his mind all thoughts of the key to the rental truck filled with his wealth, waiting to be taken to the cargo ship; all fantasies of Ferryman's baggy brown pockets where the key rested, hanging in the freezer, slowly turning from one side to another; all visions of Ferryman's blue face. In every room he searched, the policeman invited von Helden to go first, somehow managing to keep him in sight all the time while simultaneously looking at everything else. Cop skills. Even so, von Helden managed to get a look into Frida's bedside drawer without being seen. No gun. It must be downstairs, then.

The chairs and couches in the living room were draped with muslin, looking like ghosts of themselves. Von Helden turned up the rheostat that illuminated the crystal chandelier, but the effect was scarcely more wholesome somehow, merely brighter. At the policeman's request he removed and replaced the muslin drapery from every piece of furniture. This was growing tiresome. Hopefully Frida's weapon, loaded and ready to hand, would be easy to find in the dining room.

"And this is the dining room in here," he said, careful to keep the eagerness from his voice. The policeman ran his eye over the dining-room furnishings, still looking, it seemed, for a place to hide a body. He twitched the long damask tablecloth and glanced under the table.

Then, as though drawn to the fatal freezer by some sudden psychic attraction, the policeman turned his back on von Helden—his mistake, von Helden's opportunity—and headed toward the kitchen. He paused in the doorway long enough to feel along the jamb for the light switch.

Unobserved, von Helden slipped his hand inside the flatware drawer, slid his fingers over the smooth silver spoons, and felt the pistol. His hand closed over the grip; he found the trigger. Now he was the boss. With a click the policeman flooded the kitchen with light, outlining himself, making a silhouette like a fireplug.

"What time is it?"

"What?" The girl's voice woke her. Perhaps she was chattering to stay awake, now that there was enough air in the freezer to support a modest amount of chattering. Too bad about the chicken wire embedded in the glass. If not for that, they might have made a hole in the window big enough for one of them to reach out a slim little arm and undo the door latch.

"What's the time?"

Mother Grey looked at her watch, a sensible watch

with big glow-in-the-dark numbers, clearly visible even here. "Eight twenty-five."

"You're not going to tell them, are you?" came the whisper in the dark.

"Who?"

"The police when they come. I won't mention Kurt and Felicia if you don't."

"Of course I'm going to tell them." Her eyes fluttered shut.

"You're kidding, right? All you have to do is keep quiet, and your man is your own again."

"You're being silly."

"Don't tell them. Let her go." Shannon's words rang in her ears as Mother Grey fell down a long, long tunnel.

Dave Dogg was thinking, running over in his mind once more the contents of the black handbag:

One white marble hand.

One box of somebody's ashes.

A comb, a mirror, and a lipstick, Rose of Picardy, right, that was the color she wore. The smell itself was familiar, the smell of Vinnie's lips.

A prayer book, bound in morocco, initials *L.G.*

A wallet, containing a driver's license in the name of Lavinia Grey—what, was she thirty-nine? She didn't look that old—an auto registration card, various business cards, coupons for groceries, two notes to herself (one with a phone number in the 908 area), and twenty-three dollars in cash. The image of these things passed through Dave Dogg's mind in much less time than it takes to tell about it, even counting a pause to wonder about the marble hand and the ashes. Next to flash in his mind was the image of Vinnie lying dead in a heap in her good gray suit, with her little feet folded under her.

One thing was certain: Eurotrash here knew where she was. As soon as he saw Dave with the handbag, he started spouting lies about some woman priest cousin. So he knew. But how to get him to tell? Dave turned and looked at his face again, a movie-star face, expressionless in the light from the chandelier.

At least he hadn't stashed her dead body in the back of that truck. The broken-off marble hand hadn't belonged to any of the statues, either, those statues that looked so much like dead bodies wrapped up in the dark in the back of the truck. But there was something—wait a minute, Mount Outlook Cemetery was cleaned out last week, wasn't it? That's what that stuff was. So. Vinnie caught this guy with a truckload of hot statues, and he—

Why was he standing there with his hand in that drawer?

The European slid his hand out of the drawer. How about that, he was holding a gun. Again in less time than it takes to tell about it, Dave Dogg was holding a gun also, aiming it at a place slightly southwest of Eurotrash's breastbone. Eurotrash looked from the gun in his hand to Dave Dogg and back again with a puzzled frown, as if something were supposed to happen now, but he wasn't sure what.

"My cousin Frida keeps a gun in this drawer," he said, looking at it again.

"This is good," Dave Dogg said, and continued to point the nine-millimeter semiautomatic at the man's liver.

The silly laugh he gave was almost enough in itself to cause Dave Dogg to shoot him, given the circumstances.

"I agree completely," the jackass said. "My cousin is in this house alone much of the time except for my elderly aunt and uncle. In a country like this, with so much violence—"

"No, man, what I'm saying is, this is good. Because now that you have a firearm in your hand, you're putting me in peril of my life, and I can shoot your sorry ass."

"I beg your pardon?"

"You're going to die now."

"I assure you, Officer—"

"Let's understand one another. The priest who owns that handbag is the woman I love. I came here to find her. I know you know where she is. Unless I find her alive in the next two minutes, you're dead. Get it?"

17

She lay on the floor of a large cold room, sobbing uncontrollably, weeping for Stephen. She could have saved him somehow, if only she had done something slightly different, but she hadn't, and now he was dead. She would never see him again, and it was all her fault.

Strangers stood around her, but she was prostrate with grief, unable to stand, and none of the bystanders would lift a hand to help. Or they were not living. They were marble statues, all of them.

Her eyes opened. She was surprised to find them dry. Whatever crying she had been doing was dream crying. The sadness, though, was real; it sat like a lump of lead in the pit of her stomach.

Someone was chafing her hands.

"Vinnie, wake up. Wake up. Please wake up."

"Stephen," she said, but scarcely any sound came out.

"Sweetheart, it's Dave. Wake up. Don't leave me again."

"Again?" She was wide awake now. "I never left you before," she said.

"I guess you had me fooled," he said. They were out in the bright kitchen, in the warm fresh air.

"What happened?" she said. "You seem to have saved my life again."

"Anytime," he said.

Again she was aware of feet, clad this time in elegant Italian tasseled slip-ons, toes-up, not very far from her face. Dieter's feet. "What happened?" she said again.

"Oh. To him, you mean. I encouraged him to open the door to the freezer and step in, and your friend Shannon was waiting to slug him with a frozen leg of lamb. Much to my surprise. He may be out for a while."

"Good for her. I guess."

"She almost got me too. I was just a little quicker."

"She's pretty tough. Where is she?"

"In the maid's quarters, taking a hot shower."

"Did she tell you?"

"Tell me what?" So she had to tell him herself, then. And she had to speak quickly, for even as she opened her mouth to reveal the whereabouts of the fugitive newlyweds, she felt a growing temptation, a corrupt temptation, to say nothing and enjoy the results.

"About Felicia and Kurt," she said, with spasms of shivering.

He held her and rubbed her arms. "She told me you would try to tell me something about Felicia and Kurt but to pay no attention. What was she talking about?"

She had to tell him. Then it would be up to him to send whoever would stop them from boarding the plane for Saint Kitts. Kurt Smith would be arrested, leaving Felicia at loose ends and needing Dave again. Her teeth were chattering. "Just hold me for a minute," she said. And then, "What time is it?"

"I dunno. Nine thirty, maybe."

"They're gone then," she said.

"Who?"

"Your wife and her husband. Whoever. Their plane took off for Saint Kitts."

"I don't have any wife. I want you to be my wife. I'm sick and tired of chasing around after you, wondering where you are."

Many months had passed since the last time Dave asked her to marry him. Of course, she always said no. Maybe he found that discouraging. "You mean you still want to marry me?"

"Yes," he said. "Will you marry me?"

"Okay," she said.

Almost too soon, for she was happy just to lie there mindlessly in Dave's arms on the kitchen floor, sirens sounded, crowds of people came clumping in.

As they loaded her onto the gurney, the clock in the hall struck nine.

"Dave!"

"What?"

"Felicia and Kurt. They're flying to Saint Kitts. The plane takes off at nine thirty-five. You have to stop them."

"What airport?"

"I don't know. They didn't say."

"Could be Philadelphia, could be Newark, could be JFK. Right?"

"Well, yes, I suppose . . ."

"There you are then," he said. *He certainly doesn't seem to be in any hurry to catch them,* she thought. He gave her a kiss and squeezed her hand, and as the paramedics wheeled her out to one of the waiting ambulances, it struck her that Dave Dogg was no more eager to have Felicia come back than Mother Grey herself was.

She was shivering uncontrollably. "Really, I'm fine," she said. They swathed her in blankets and told her just to take it easy.

With a jolt and a wail of the siren, they took off down the road. She gazed at the ceiling of the ambulance, thinking, *Now I have to plan a wedding.*

In its own good time the law began the process of gathering in all the Smiths, their spouses, and their servants from the four corners of the earth and determining the guilt or innocence of each. Felicia and Kurt were able to honeymoon for a week and a half before the authorities tracked them down. Wilson was never found, at least in connection with the cemetery robbery. Liesl got somebody other than Dieter von Helden to back her film, which won a prize the following year at the Cannes Film Festival and became a minor cult hit. They never showed European art movies in the prison where von Helden was serving out his life sentence for murder, and so at least he was spared the humiliation of having to watch it.

* * *

And what of Mark Smith?

His daughter Shannon picked him up at the county jail shortly after midnight, so that he would not have to spend the night in jail. In order to do this, she was forced to endure a number of ordeals.

First of all, when she got out of the maid's shower, there was nothing to put on but the maid's clothes. The maid was a little short woman.

Then there was the trial of the felon's pockets. Von Helden, stretched unconscious on the Smith kitchen floor, had the key to her rental car in his clothes. When Shannon explained this to Detective Dave Dogg, he made believe he didn't hear her but stared at the kitchen ceiling, whistling. Luckily she found it almost at once. Every time she put her hand in another pocket, she expected von Helden to wake up and grab her by the arm.

The next trial was to run the gauntlet of stares in the lobby of the hotel in Fishersville, filled even at eleven o'clock at night with well-dressed tourists from Manhattan, none of whom seemed to have anything better to do than to give her the eye as she walked in wearing a truncated maid's uniform and clogs. She could never recall the experience afterward without shuddering.

She told herself it was all grist for her mill. Someday she would make a book out of it. The most important thing was that she was able to rescue her father, this time at least. Whether he would stay rescued, or whether he would need more rescuing after they went home to Phoenix, only time would tell.

How crazy was he? Martine Wellworth's psychiatrist never did get a chance to check him over. Back at the hotel all he would say was that he wanted to go home.

She wanted to tell him about James W. Smith, how

he had another family, how he had survived into his old age, only to become unreachably demented. She began with Mrs. Weeds and the letters from Nana. "So then I went to Pennsylvania with Mother Grey."

"Tell me about it in the morning, sweetheart," he said. "I'm very tired now." He had understood nothing she said. Or maybe he didn't want to understand. Maybe she should leave it alone and tell him when he was stronger.

Or never tell him.

They fell into their beds. Not until the following day did Shannon remember Nana's ashes.

Mother Grey brought the box of ashes to the hotel after church. She had managed to bounce out of her hospital bed just in time for the ten-thirty Eucharist at St. Bede's. She found the Smiths packing again, or repacking, Mark fussing over the folding and placement of garments in his bag. That very afternoon they planned to head back to Phoenix.

"Nana!" Shannon said. She held the box out and looked at it; her face fell as though the magic had gone out of it. "I don't know what to do with her now." She sounded almost like her grandfather, lost, purposeless.

"Do you still have the shovel in your bag?"

"Yes, I do."

"Let's go, then."

And so they left Mark behind in the hotel, madly packing, and went up on Mount Outlook to the St. Joseph's cemetery, high on the hill. They climbed the fence and found the place where the Fitzroys were buried, Mary Agnes's grandmother and grandfather and the others. There, among the new blades of grass pushing up through the moist earth, they planted Nana.

"Do you think Father de Spain will mind?"

"Not if he never hears about it," Mother Grey said. The priest at Mary Agnes's parish church in Phoenix had already performed a Roman Catholic funeral service for her. Mother Grey said some other prayers appropriate to the occasion—surely Father de Spain wouldn't really mind—and they dropped the box into the hole. After they put the sod back, you could hardly tell the ground had been disturbed, except for a little hump.

"This is a beautiful cemetery," said Shannon. "I know Nana would like to be here."

"Will you ever come back?"

"I'll come every year and put flowers on her grave. Without my dad, though. He's never coming back to New Jersey, he says."

"I'll miss you, Shannon," Mother Grey said, and gave her a hug. "Don't forget to write. The next time you find the great love of your life, make sure he's someone nice."

"Hey. Live and learn. You know, I thought that policeman was the great love of my life when he let us out of the freezer."

Mother Grey said, "No, he's the great love of mine." To say so gave her enormous pleasure.

"Can I come to your wedding?"

"Absolutely." That made, let's see, seventy-one guests so far, seventy-two if Mark came, but no, he was never coming east again, he said. So seventy-one. It was time to think about reserving the fire hall and hiring a caterer. My word, the expense.